D0680858

If Your Girl Only Knew

Also by Dwayne S. Joseph

Choices Men Make
The Womanizers
Never Say Never

Anthologies:
Around the Way Girls
Gigolos Get Lonely Too

If Your Girl Only Knew

Dwayne S. Joseph

URBAN BOOKS LLC
www.urbanbooks.net

Urban Books LLC
10 Brennan Place
Deer Park, NY 11729

Copyright ©2005 Dwayne S. Joseph

All rights reserved. No part of this book may be reproduced in any form or by any means without prior consent of the Publisher, excepting brief quotes used in reviews.

ISBN 1-893196-64-X

First Printing September 2006
Printed in the United States of America

10 9 8 7 6 5 4 3 2 1

This is a work of fiction. Any references or similarities to actual events, real people, living, or dead, or to real locales are intended to give the novel a sense of reality. Any similarity in other names, characters, places, and incidents is entirely coincidental.

Submit Wholesale Orders to:
Kensington Publishing Corp.
C/O Penguin Group (USA) Inc.
Attention: Order Processing
405 Murray Hill Parkway
East Rutherford, NJ 07073-2316
Phone: 1-800-526-0275
Fax: 1-800-227-9604

Dedicated to everyone's first and true loves.

"The time is right to make old friends."

—Anonymous-

Acknowledgments

This is a work of fiction! Nothing in this book has happened in real life. I am not the main character. I did not bump into my ex. This is a work of fiction! I had to get that out of the way, because I know that everyone is going to assume this story is real. But, trust me, it's not.

God: Thanks once again for being there.

Wendy and my daughters, Tatiana & Natalia: You are my world.

To my family: Mom, Dad, Daren (yeah, my lil bro produced Juelz Santana's track, "The Whistle Song"! That's him whistling and everything!) Teens, Evan, Granny, Grand-mother, Lourdes, Russell, Ivan, Grace, Prianna, Leila. . . . Love you guys!

My cousins: Too many to name—thanks for the love and support. Kirt . . . You know I'm here, kid.

To my peeps for life: Chris, Lisa, Jessie, Jasmine, Gregg, Kristie, Tho, Sathy, Micah, Tiffany, Layla, Brian, Mia, Carlos, Mariana, Scott, Monique, Zoe, Eric Pete, La Jill Hunt. Love for all of you! Suzette Harrison, can't wait to read the new book!

To the Urban Books staff: Thanks for caring about your authors.

Robilyn Heath—still there, always there. Thank You!

Thank you, Portia, for your guidance and support.

To the readers: What can I say? THANK YOU a thousand times for the support you all have shown me. I truly, truly appreciate all of the meetings, the e-mails, and the feedback! I hope you all enjoy! Big thanks to Shirley Merrills, Mario Merrills, and Kayra Alvarado.

Patricia and the rest of the members of Baltimore Readers with W.I.S.D.O.M.

Tammy Gholston, Nancy Silvas and the rest of the members of Aminia Latrese Carter and the rest of the members of African American Sisters in Spirit.

Nalo Ervin and the rest of the members of Women in Me.

Lonnie and the rest of the members of Ujima Nia.

Marie and the rest of the members of the Circle of Sisters.

Jackie, Courtney and the rest of the members of The Sweet Soul Sisters.

Lisa and the rest of the members of In the Company of My Sisters. (I couldn't make it to the meeting, but you chose my book to discuss and I appreciate that).

Gwenn and the rest of the members of Cushcity.com.

Alicia and the rest of the members of One Book @ A Time.

I enjoyed meeting with all of you and hope to do it again to discuss all of the drama I've conjured up in this tale.

To my New York Giants: Division champs in '05. We're Super Bowl-bound, baby!

Dwayne S. Joseph—Djoseph21044@yahoo.com

If Your Girl Only Knew

Prologue

Jocelyn.

She was whispering my name as she stood before me naked, swaying her hips rhythmically to music that only she could hear. Her dance was slow, hypnotic, and arousing, and made bumps rise from my skin. She traced a finger from inside of her mouth and dragged it down in between her breast, licked her lips and smiled.

Whispering my name seductively again, she came toward me slowly, grabbed hold of my throbbing member, straddled me, and slid me inside of her. I exhaled from the warmth and wetness of her.

Little by little, my body began to move in tune with hers, until we were both dancing to the same sexual groove. Up and down. Back and forth. In circles.

We danced passionately this way for what seemed like hours. As her movements became more intense, I could feel myself nearing the point of explosion. I tried as hard as I could to hold it back, but with her fire, I couldn't, and I released powerfully.

Seconds after that I felt her buckle on top of me with her own climax. "Oh, David!"

I quickly opened my eyes at the sound of my fiancée's voice, Janelle. She was naked above me and breathing heavily. Her dark-chocolate skin was coated with a light sheen of perspiration. I was naked and covered with sweat too.

"David," she whispered, "that was incredible. Baby, what got into you? I can't remember the last time you were so intense."

I shrugged my shoulders but didn't respond.

Thankfully Janelle didn't wait for a response. She kissed me on my neck and lips, then rose from on top of me and walked off into the bathroom. She closed the door behind her.

I sat up and dragged my hands down over my face. "Jocelyn," I whispered. "Damn."

I couldn't believe that just happened. Jocelyn Alvarez. My ex. My first love. The one that I always felt "got away." She'd been on my mind constantly ever since I ran into her a month ago back in Philly when I was there for a book signing. I hadn't seen her since we broke up six years ago.

Our breakup hadn't been pretty. Dating since we were sixteen, I turned twenty-one and fucked up by cheating on her with her rival, Theresa Cueves.

Jocelyn and Theresa were like oil and water; they just didn't mix. They'd hated each other since before I came into the picture.

Apparently back in junior high, Jocelyn had stolen Theresa's boyfriend. I guess Theresa had been looking for revenge ever since then, and like a fool, even though I knew how Jocelyn felt about her, I helped Theresa get it. I got all caught up in Theresa's firm breasts and J.-Lo-like ass, and had sex with her at a party that Jocelyn, who was supposed to be away for the weekend, ended up coming to.

In my defense, I was drunk. But that didn't matter. Jocelyn dumped me on the spot, and no matter how hard I tried, no matter what I said or did, she wouldn't take me back. That was the worst.

Jocelyn was my everything. Ask me who my ideal woman was in both looks and personality, and Jocelyn's name would have been the one coming from my lips. My moment of drunken weakness with Theresa was a major slip-up that I would never forgive myself for. I dated other females after Jocelyn, but none of them ever gave me the feeling that Jocelyn gave me. Not even Janelle, who I'd been with for the past year and a half. *Damn,* I thought to myself. *That dream was just too intense, too real.* I shook my head. I should never have sent Jocelyn that e-mail.

After bumping into her, we spent almost three hours reminiscing and filling each other in on the happenings in each other's lives. After what I'd done, and the way Jocelyn had swore she'd never talk to me again, the last thing I expected was just to be talking as though I'd never been a fool. But there we were, talking, smiling, laughing, staring. We gazed into each other's eyes so many times, even if we wanted to, there was no denying that the spark still existed between us.

Before we parted, we exchanged e-mail addresses, with the intent of keeping in touch with one another occasionally. We were both busy after all—me as an author, and she as an exec in advertising. So once in a while should have been all the time we had. Besides, I was engaged—something I hadn't told Jocelyn—so my time was definitely limited.

Once in a while is how things started initially. I'd e-mail her and say hi. She'd email me and say bye. Nothing's wrong with that, right?

But a couple of weeks ago, I was at home alone, supposedly to work on my new book, when I did something that I shouldn't have done. Something that would have major repercussions. Sitting in front of my laptop, I e-mailed Jocelyn and bared my soul.

Even though we were apart for all these years, I'd never

truly gotten over her. Like I said, she was my ideal partner. Bumping into her only brought feelings which I'd tried to bury back to the surface.

That night, alone with my laptop, everything came to a head, and I started typing. And then I hit send. And now here I was, having incredible sex with my fiancée, only it wasn't my fiancée I was sexing. Damn. It's a good thing I didn't call out Jocelyn's name.

When Janelle came out of the bathroom, like a woman in love, she wrapped her arms around me, kissed me, and pulled me down on the mattress to cuddle. Eventually with her head on my shoulder, she fell asleep.

As for me, I couldn't sleep. I just lay in bed, staring up at the ceiling. I sent the e-mail. Damn. She hadn't yet, but how was Jocelyn going to respond? And even more important, what would she say when I told her about Janelle, which I knew I had to do sooner or later.

When Sleeping Dogs Lie

David

I lifted the seventy-five-pound dumbbell above my head for the sixth time and then lowered it slowly to the floor. My chest muscles were burning from the exertion as sweat trickled down my forehead in rivers. I took a deep breath, picked up my towel, and wiped the hard-earned perspiration away.

"Yo, I got something to tell you," I huffed, rising from the bench. I took another deep breath; it was another hard, solid workout. Standing beside me, waiting to do his own set of six, was my boy, Marc, who I'd known since second grade.

"What's up?" he asked, lying back on the bench.

Marc's a six-two tank who thrives on having the perfect body. He lives by the whole my-body-is-my-temple credo. He even owns two gyms in the city and is a part-time personal trainer. If it were up to him, McDonald's would only be a last name, and Wendy's would be nothing more than a girl he'd conquered.

It was because of his persistence that I began working out. I used to be a one forty-five lover-boy with a few muscles. Now that I'd followed Marc's workout and diet regimen, I was lean at one seventy-five, with a six-pack of abdominals to wash clothes on. I was proud of what I'd done with my body and so were the ladies, who gave me more than enough stares to keep my head gassed up.

"You know how I've been e-mailing back and forth with Jocelyn sometimes?" I said, settling in behind the bench to spot him for his set. He was pressing one hundred and twenty pounds. *One day I too will be up there in the land of the big boys.* For now, I was stuck at one hundred and ten.

"Yeah," Marc grunted out, as he pushed the dumbbells into the air.

I watched carefully and spotted him by the elbows.

His movements were smooth, controlled and almost rhythmic. It was only after the sixth repetition that he finally needed me to help him force out an additional two reps. After a loud yell, he dropped the dumbbells to the ground and sat up, "What about it?" he asked, breathing heavily.

I hesitated for a second; I could already imagine his reaction. "Well, a couple of weeks ago I did something crazy."

Marc gave me an "uh-oh" look. "What did you do?"

"I told her that I was still in love with her."

"What?" Marc looked at me like I was crazy. Shit, maybe I was. "What do you mean you told her you were still in love with her? Please tell me that you're kidding."

I shook my head. "Nah man, I'm not."

"Bruh, are you crazy? How can you still be in love with Jocelyn? Do you have any idea how ridiculous that sounds?"

"I know man, but . . ."

"But nothing, bruh. You and Jocelyn dated way, way back in high school. Y'all been apart all this time. There's no way in hell you can still be in love with her. Shit, you two haven't exchanged that many e-mails. I know because I've read them."

"I know it sounds crazy, man," I said, shrugging my shoulders. "But, believe it or not, I am still feeling her."

"Come on, Dave. The only thing you're feeling is that little head of yours swell when you read her boring-ass e-mails.

You're engaged to be married, man. Damn. I can't believe you're tripping like this. I can't believe you told her that you're in love with her. That's bananas, man. You're tripping over some 'young love' shit."

"Man, how many times do I have to tell you that what Jocelyn and I had wasn't just young love. Man, it was real and it was true. Shit, if I wouldn't have fucked up, we'd still be together today."

"Come on, bruh, you don't know that."

"Nah, I do, man. You weren't there when we ran into each other again. You weren't there to see the sparks that still exist. I was. I know it sounds crazy, man, but I'm telling you I did the right thing by letting her know how I feel about her."

Marc stood up and grabbed his towel and wiped the sweat off his face. "'The right thing,' huh? Damn, man. I just don't understand how you could say you're still in love with her. Six years, bruh."

"I know it sounds strange, man, but I've never gotten over her."

"Bruh . . ."

"Hear me out, man. Jocelyn has always had everything I wanted in a woman—beauty, brains, style, great personality—everything. She is the very definition of complete. I was at my best when I was with her. Shit, she made me want to be the best. I've never had a relationship as intense with another woman as I had with Jocelyn."

"Of course not, man. Jocelyn was your first love. That's when love is supposed to be the most intense."

"So if you understand me, why are you flipping out on me?"

"You didn't let me finish, bruh. I said that's when love is supposed to be the most intense, not the most gratifying, fulfilling, or special. Love is a drug, man. And every day fools like you walk around searching for that ultimate high that they experienced the first time. But you know what? They never find it. And you want to know why?" He paused and looked at me as we headed upstairs to do our cardio workout.

"Why?"

"Because no matter what you do, or who you fall in love with, love will never be as intense as it was when you felt it for that first time. So you can save the 'never-had-a-relationship-as-intense' bit, because you wouldn't have had one anyway. Now, having proved my point, you can let that shit with Jocelyn go. She may not have been my favorite person at first, but I can say without a doubt that Janelle's the one for you. She's the one you wanna be putting your focus on."

"Man, Janelle is a special woman, but I don't know about her being the one."

"You don't know? Bruh, she's wearing an engagement ring that you gave her, which meant that at some point, she had to be 'the one.'"

"Yeah, I know," I said, hopping on the bike for my workout. "But we've been having some problems."

"Since when?" Marc asked, pedaling slowly. "Since Jocelyn came back in the picture? Bruh, you better get your mind right and focus on marrying Janelle and let your idle fantasies go."

"Whatever, man," I said, pedaling harder.

I was frustrated over the things he'd said. I know he meant well, but he just didn't understand. Marc never felt love before because he'd always been too busy trying to win the playa of the year award.

"It's not a fantasy, man. Something is still there between me and Jocelyn. And whether you agree or not, I'm not willing to let her go again without seeing if she feels the same."

Marc stopped pedaling and looked at me. "You're for real about this, huh?"

"Yeah, man."

"Damn, bruh."

"Something's there, man."

"But you're engaged."

"I know. But if I'm gonna get married, I want to make sure it's to the right woman."

Marc shrugged his shoulders and started pedaling again. "As crazy as you might be, I can't argue with that logic."

"I just don't want to miss out on an opportunity."

"Yeah, I got you. I got you."

"Thank you."

We pedaled in silence for the next couple of minutes until Marc looked over at me again. "Yo bruh, let me ask you something."

"What's up?" I said breathlessly. I always hated doing cardio exercises.

"Did you ever have that discussion with Jocelyn that you were supposed to have?"

I hesitated before I answered.

Marc had stopped pedaling now and was looking down on me. It had been a few days, but I knew he was gonna ask me this sooner or later.

The discussion that I was supposed to have had with Jocelyn was about our mates. Although we'd spoken several times via e-mail, I'd never mentioned Janelle's existence. I didn't do it intentionally at first. I was just so caught up in reminiscing and catching up with her that it just slipped my mind. I knew I had to sooner or later though. And I was going to. But then I felt myself falling all over again for her, and I decided not to because I didn't want to give her a reason to back away.

As for whether or not she was seeing anyone, I had no clue. She never mentioned a friend, a fiancé, a husband—nothing. And I didn't ask. I didn't want to know. Besides, she would have told me, right?

"Not yet," I said.

"Why not?"

I got off of my bike and wiped sweat from my forehead. "I don't know, man. It just never came up."

"'Never came up'? Damn, man, I could understand you keeping Janelle under wraps, but aren't you the least bit curious to know if she's seeing someone. I mean, shit, man, for all you know, she could be married."

"Nah, she's not."

"How do you know?"

"When we met back in Philly, I scoped her finger for a ring. She didn't have one on."

"So? Man, she could have been having it cleaned or repaired. You better ask her, man. Shit, you should have asked before you started sending out love letters."

"All right, man," I said, walking off toward the water fountain. I'd had enough of his lecturing.

Marc came up beside me. "Look, bruh, I don't mean to give you a hard time over this. It's cool if you feel like you still got something with Jocelyn. I mean, shit, as much as you two were in love back in high school, it'd be all right to see you two together again. I'm just saying, before you even start walking down memory lane, you should get some shit out in the open."

"Yeah, I know, man. I guess I just didn't want to make her run off."

"You gotta give her a chance to make that decision, man. Hey, if the sparks are there like you say they are, maybe she won't care about Janelle. As for yourself, before you go and get yourself killed by some jealous boyfriend or husband, find out what her situation is."

"And what if she has someone?"

Marc shrugged. "That's up to you, bruh. You know my policy about chicks with dudes. I don't give a fuck how fine the woman is—I ain't fucking with her. But I don't go looking for love. I just want to smash it and run. You're the one talking the love game. And that's a whole other ballgame. If she's got someone, you have to decide for yourself if the sparks you felt are worth any headache that another dude might bring."

I nodded my head. He was right. "I'll e-mail and ask her tonight, man. Will that make you happy?"

"Hey, don't do it for me, bruh. I don't give a fuck either way. But, just out of curiosity, if she has a man, what are you gonna do?"

Marc didn't wait for my answer and walked off. Obviously, that question was more for me to mull over than to respond to.

What am I going to do? I asked myself that question as warm water sprayed over me. I was standing in my shower at home, staring at the ceramic tiling. *What am I going to do?* I know I felt that the sparks were real, and that we still had a connection, but was I willing to go after her still if she had someone? I turned off the shower, grabbed my towel, and stepped out of the shower, asking myself that question.

After drying off, I stepped into the bedroom and met Janelle. She was standing beside the bed, unbuttoning her blouse.

"You're home early," I said, slipping into a pair of boxers.

"No, I'm home late."

" 'Late'? What are you late for?"

Janelle looked up at me. "David, did you forget about our reservations?"

" 'Reservations'?"

"Yes, at the Blue Lagoon. We're meeting Jeff and Renea there for dinner at eight."

"Did you tell me this?"

"I told you before I went out for drinks the other night."

"It must have slipped my mind."

"Everything just seems to be slipping your mind lately."

I was busy selecting a pair of black slacks from the closet. "Let's not start anything, okay. I've had a good day and I'm not in the mood."

Janelle cut her eyes at me. "You're never in the mood. Not unless it requires sitting in front of that damn laptop."

"Look, let's just get dressed and go out and try to have a good time. We had this talk already. I'm a writer. The laptop and I go hand in hand."

"Right, so the fiancée has to sit and wait her turn," Janelle snapped.

"Janelle, goddamn! Can't we just have one night without arguing, please? Can we just go out and have a good time?"

Janelle hmph'd. "I'm surprised you're not backing out so you and your laptop can be alone."

I dragged my hands down over my face and then turned away from her and went to the closet and selected a navy blue shirt. The last thing I felt like doing was arguing.

When I told Marc we'd been having problems, I wasn't lying. We had been. Most of that was my fault. I guess I was just feeling a little pressure about the coming wedding, and I started to distance myself. It's not that I didn't want to marry Janelle, it was just that she kept talking about it. It was like I couldn't go a day without hearing the *M* word. I was coming to grips with it though. As much as the constant talk irked me, I couldn't deny that I was happy and ready to be with Janelle.

But then I bumped into Jocelyn.

Marc was right—that's when our real problems started.

David

When Janelle and I got back from the restaurant, I couldn't sleep. I was too stressed because, once again, we had put on our facade of being the perfect couple in public while, in private, it was a different story altogether. On the way to the restaurant we argued. First it was about being late, then it was about which radio station would be played. Who knows what petty things we argued about after that. All I know is we went at it from our home to our car, in the car on the way, and then from the car to the restaurant's front doors. Our act began when we stepped inside.

My arguing with Janelle wasn't the only thing keeping me up though. Truth be told, I was busy thinking about Jocelyn too. Marc's last question really stuck with me. What would I do if she did have someone in her life?

As much as I didn't want to know, Marc was right: I had to know. And Jocelyn had to know about Janelle. What she would do, I didn't know. But the secret had to come out.

I turned my head and looked at Janelle as she slept soundlessly beside me. She hadn't bothered to kiss me goodnight like she normally did, and I couldn't blame her. What was happening between us wasn't her fault at all.

I got out of bed slowly and left the room. Now was as good a time as any to get everything out in the open. Sitting in the living room, I opened my laptop and logged onto my e-mail. I skimmed quickly through my inbox, searching for only one thing—mail from Jocelyn. Guess what? It was waiting for me at the bottom.

My heart started to beat heavily as I stared at her name. This was what I'd been waiting for, yet dreading at the same time. I hesitated for a moment before double-clicking on the message. *Come on, Dave,* I thought to myself. *There's no turning back now.*

I took a quick glance down the hall toward the bedroom. Janelle was still sleeping; I could hear her breathing. After a deep breath and another slight hesitation, I exhaled and double-clicked the message.

David,

Wow. That's what I said after reading your e-mail. David, I don't know what to say. I'm in shock right now. You're still in love with me. That's a pretty heavy thing to digest. I mean, what am I supposed to say to that? After all of our years apart, I never expected to see you again. But there we were—both in Philadelphia for different reasons, bumping into each other. You said that our meeting again was destiny. That we'd been guided to that very spot on South Street that very moment. I don't know, David. I do believe that all things happen for a reason, but were we guided there? I guess the answer to that is pointless now. We met again and that's all that matters. David, before I go on, there's something that I need to tell you. Why I didn't mention this before, I don't know. Or maybe I do. Maybe I was feeling the same thing you were. Maybe I didn't want to scare you away. Maybe that's why I kept this secret from you until now. What I'm trying to say, David, is that I'm married.

I stopped reading and lifted my head. *Did she just say that she was married?* I looked down and read it again.

What I'm trying to say, David, is that I'm married.

I looked up again. She *was* married. But there was more. I looked down and kept reading.

I'm sure your mouth dropped open after that bombshell. Believe me, I know I should have said something sooner. I don't really know why I didn't, other than to say that maybe there's some truth to what you said about us being led to meet again after all this time. I'm married, David, but I'll be honest—your e-mail really helped me admit something to myself that I've been trying to deny for the longest time. I'm married, but I'm not happy. I haven't been for a while now. I've basically been going through the motions of marriage, fulfilling the duties that a wife is supposed to fill because I'd sworn to do that. I was pretty much resigned to do that, but then we had our reunion. Since that day everything's changed for me. I think about you a lot, David. I have been since our first meeting. I've thought a lot about the love that we shared back when we were younger. I remember how good it felt to be together, and how you always made me smile. I know we were young, but we had a real love. A love that I haven't felt since. I can't top your e-mail, David, because I'm still a little confused inside. But I know that I still have feelings for you. Strong ones. I'm not happy, David. But I'd like to be. Maybe we should meet again. Let me know your thoughts. Oh, and before I let you go—are you involved with anyone? I revealed my secret, now it's your turn—if you have one that is. (I guess we should have asked these questions before we jumped off the edge, huh?)

Always,
Jocelyn

I closed the laptop and exhaled slowly. She was unhappily married and she wanted to meet again. I leaned my head back on the sofa and looked up at the ceiling. This was surreal. She didn't say that she was in love with me, but her wanting to see me was good enough.

I sat up and lifted the laptop cover. I looked back toward the bedroom again and listened for Janelle's breathing. Satisfied that she wouldn't be coming out any time soon, I clicked on new memo. It was now time to tell her about Janelle.

Janelle

I wasn't really asleep when David walked out of the room. I just kept my eyes closed so that he would think I was and leave. I was actually glad that he'd decided to get out of bed because I didn't really feel like being around him. Besides, I hated when we lay in bed with our backs to one another anyway. I didn't know what was going on with him, but he'd really changed. He'd become more detached. I know what you're thinking—there must have been another woman. I'll admit, that crossed my mind once. But as quickly as that thought came, it went away. I trusted my man. And he'd never given me a reason not to.

I loved David with all my heart. I'd never met a man who made me feel the way he did. David was a rare brother to find. He wasn't on the corner doing the hustle. He didn't have any baby momma drama going on in his life because he didn't have any kids. Best of all, he was fine, intelligent, driven, and wasn't concerned with trying to be a playa's playa.

It took me a little while, but I eventually agreed to move in with him. After all, he'd passed all of my necessary tests. He could handle his money, he was determined to succeed, his momma taught him the right way to treat a black woman and, best of all, my momma and daddy loved him. My momma always thought David and I were special together, and almost from day one, she wanted to know when we were going to have kids. Even my daddy, as over-protective as he could be, wanted to know.

Before David, I'd never really thought about having kids. My career was too important to me, and I didn't want anything slowing me down. But with David in my life, the prospect of being a wife and a mother was starting to look good.

I met David at Marc's party. I didn't know Marc at the time, but my date for the evening knew him from the gym he went to, which I later found out Marc owned. I didn't really want to go, but I didn't want to be home alone on New Year's Eve either. I had just moved to New York from California because of a position and salary that I couldn't refuse, so I didn't really know too many people. I wasn't looking forward to leaving the sunshine behind to live in the city that never slept, where people's attitudes were as rough as sandpaper, but I was excited about the change of scenery. I was also ready to move out from under my family's wing and branch out on my own. Of course I did have several bouts with homesickness and at times wondered if I'd made the right decision to leave.

Especially when the temperature dropped.

You know a California-born and -bred sister didn't like that. The cold was something entirely new for me. The East Coast winter was enough to make a sister want to leave. My idea of cold was anything below seventy degrees, so when the holidays came, you know I was more than ready to go back home for Christmas.

It was nice being back in the warmth visiting with my family and friends. It seemed like the excitement waited to happen until after I left. I found out who was pregnant, who was sleeping with whose baby-daddy, who went to jail and who came out of jail; so and so was divorcing so and so, he said, she said, she cried, he lied. I had a lot of catching up to do.

Unfortunately I never got a chance to catch up on anything, as my vacation was cut short when my boss called and told me that he needed me to come in to work the day after Christmas. I pouted about it to my parents, a luxury of being back home, and then called the airport to change my return flight.

When I got back to New York, snow was just beginning to fall. Having lived in Cali all my life, I had never seen snow in person before, so when the plane landed, I got off, grabbed my luggage, braved the weather and stood outside of the airport to wait for a cab. While I did, I watched the snow pile on the ground, shook my head, and asked myself how I could leave California for this.

I had to admit the snow looked beautiful as it was falling. I mean, I wasn't going to build a snowman or anything, or go sledding down the block, but it was nice to see. I admired the snowfall all the way home and even into the night from my window. But my admiration stopped there. The snow was pretty until I had to struggle my way through it to get to work the next day. Walking through and around slush puddles, with my feet all cold and wet, I had to ask myself again why I'd left Cali.

What made things even worse for me was that, being new, I didn't really have anyone to share my pain with. At work, I was one of only a few minorities, and not everyone was as down as I would have liked. The rest of my co-workers were white. And you know how they feel about the cold. Or, should I say, don't feel the cold.

Anyway, my phone bill was already sky-high from calling and venting to everyone back home, so when New Year's came around, saying yes to my date, some guy whose name I don't even remember, was out of desperation. I think I spent all of five minutes with my nameless date, who couldn't spell the word *rhythm* if you gave him the letters in order.

After having my toes stepped on one time too many, I dismissed my date and disappeared to find a drink. Being alone amongst strangers was definitely better than the foot surgery I had been enduring on the floor. I lost count of the number of times I had asked myself why I was in New York, and after my second lonely glass of wine, I decided to call it a night and bring in the New Year alone.

But then David stepped through the door.

"Tina, girl, I been hit in the head with a bag of nickels!"

After meeting David, I had to call my best friend the next day. Tina Jordan and I were complete opposites. She liked to live the glamorous lifestyle, without the hard work required, while I didn't mind getting my hands dirty. That's why she married Derrick Dickinson.

Derrick breathed Tina back in high school. He wasn't the best looking, or the most interesting brother, but he was sweet. And smart. And those brains paid off for him. He started an Internet company straight out of high school and became a millionaire before turning twenty-one. Tina married him one year later, and although she never admitted it, I know she loved him.

Of course, even with his money, he still couldn't get fifth place in a contest based on his looks, but he treated her like a queen and that's what mattered. They lived in a ten-bedroom mansion in Hollywood with an indoor pool and a sauna. They went to big bashes and had famous friends. Tina was quite happy.

"'Hit in the head with a bag of nickels'? What are you talking about, girl?" Tina asked.

"That's slang for *I met a man.*"

"Girl, you didn't?"

"I did," I said with the biggest smile I'd had in a long time.

"Girl, I can see you cheesin' from all the way over here. As much as your lonely ass been callin' me these past couple of months, blowing up my phone, you better give me details. Speak!"

I laughed and flopped down on my bed. "Girl, I swear I have never seen a man as incredibly attractive as David. He has these brown eyes that are mysterious and intense. His smile could make butter melt, and his lips are finer than L.L.'s."

"It's like that?"

"It's like that. I met him at a party I went to. Girl, remind me to tell you about my date, but anyway, he came in wearing a black turtleneck and black dress pants, looking like Morris Chestnut with curls. Sex appeal, girl! He was funkin' it up."

"I see," Tina said with envy in her tone. "So, tell me more."

"Well, I don't know how long I stood in a trance just staring, but eventually, somebody accidentally bumped into me and brought me back to reality. Of course I didn't want to seem like I was all into him, so I held it down and slid into a corner of the room and checked him out. Girl, the East Coast wind couldn't have stopped me from sweating. Hot, you hear me?"

"I'm hearing, I'm hearing."

"Anyway, as the countdown began—"

"Wait a minute," Tina said cutting me off. "You were alone then? What happened to Mr. Wonderful?"

"I'm gettin' there, girl, keep your bra on. Anyway, like I was saying, as the countdown began he came up to me with two glasses of champagne in his hand. He introduced himself, handed me a glass, and said something about not celebrating alone. I didn't really hear him though because I was too busy tryin' not to orgasm."

"Oooh, girl!"

"Yes, Tina. It was like that."

"Then what? Speak, speak!"

I slammed my hand down on my mattress and laughed out loud. "Well, after the countdown was over and the confetti settled, we began to talk. Girl, his voice . . . mmm. He invited me out for breakfast after the party. We went and talked for hours. Tina, imagine how surprised I was when he told me he was a writer!"

"Dayum! For real? 'A writer'? You're an editor!"

"I know. That tripped me out too."

After giving her the rest of the details, and then telling her about the guy with two left feet, I hung up the phone, lay back on the bed, and thought about David.

Everything took off for us after that. We moved in together after six months of dating. Actually, I moved in with him.

Until David came along, the whole living-happily-ever-after concept had never been a reality for me. Never one to settle with just anybody; I had been single for a long time. Being single was just fine with me because I was never the type to rely on anyone to bring sunshine to my world. But then David came along and brought me true happiness.

That all seemed like ages ago, though. I just wished I could figure out what was going on with him. I knew he was working on a new book, which he still hadn't shared with me, which was very surprising, since he always talked about his books with me. Maybe he was just really preoccupied with his writing. After all, he did have a deadline to meet.

I wish I could have put everything in reverse and gone the other way. I was so tired of our arguing. Just the smallest things turned into fights where one of us ended up leaving and the other slammed doors.

Of course, we did the kiss and make up thing, but as good as the sex was, that was getting tired too. We just seemed to become like two strangers, and with each day that passed by, David became more and more distant.

I may have been frustrated with some of the things that had been happening in our relationship, but I still loved him and I couldn't imagine being without him.

Did he feel the same way about me?

Did he want what I wanted?

Was our marriage still important to him?

Those and other questions ran through my mind day after day. What scared me the most was that I didn't like the answers I had been coming up with.

David

"She's married."

Marc looked up at me from his plate of chicken and mashed potatoes. "What?"

"She's married," I said again.

"Who's married?"

"Jocelyn?"

Marc dropped his fork. "Are you serious?"

"As a heart attack," I said.

"When'd you find out?"

"She e-mailed me two nights ago."

"Damn, bruh. Sorry to hear that. I mean, I'm not gonna front, I wasn't for you trying to get with her, but I know you had your heart set on it. Oh well, don't sweat it too hard. You still got a fine woman at your side. Hey, at least you got to fantasize a little."

He picked up his fork and gathered some food. Just as he was about to slip it into his mouth, I cleared my throat and said, "I wasn't finished, man."

Marc's fork came to a dead stop right in front of his open

mouth. Looking at me he said, "What do you mean, you weren't finished?"

"Remember when you asked me what I was going to do if she was involved?"

"Yeah," Marc said, the tone in his voice obviously not liking where I was going.

"Well, I made a decision."

"Really?"

"Yeah. Actually, she made it for me."

"She did? And what decision did she make?"

Marc's fork was back on the plate, while his eyes stayed glued on me. I knew he wasn't going to like my answer, but I didn't care. I'd been on a high ever since that e-mail.

"We're gonna meet, and we're gonna see what happens."

"What?" Marc said it so loud that other diners around us looked over in our direction. Marc excused himself for his outburst and then in a lower voice said, "What do you mean, you're gonna see what happens? Dave, she's fucking married."

"Yeah, but not happily."

"That doesn't matter, bruh. She's still married."

"I know that, man."

"You know that, huh? Then what the fuck are you talking about you guys are gonna meet? Man, I knew you were tripping, but I didn't realize you'd already fallen and busted your head. Does she even know about Janelle yet?"

"If she read my reply back to her, she does."

Marc sat back in his seat. "So then there's still a chance this may not happen. I mean once she finds out about Janelle, she'll probably back off."

I shrugged my shoulders. I thought about the possibility of her backing off, but I didn't see it happening. "I don't know, man. After the things she said, I think she'll still want to meet."

"Damn, Dave, y'all are both tripping."

"Hey, man, it's love."

"Yeah, yeah, spare me the sappy explanation."

"I'm just saying, Marc."

"Yeah, whatever. Anyway, let me ask you—what happens if you two do end up meeting?"

"What do you mean?"

"I mean where will you take things from there?"

"I don't know, man. I guess the first step will be for us to just sit and talk and figure out what we both want and need. After that, who knows?"

"Bruh, Jocelyn's a married woman. It doesn't matter that she's unhappy. Steps? What steps are you talking about? Breaking up her marriage?"

"I won't be breaking up anything if that's what she wants."

"Come on, Dave, keep it real. You're talking about coming in between a man and his wife."

"Marc, will you chill. I said we're gonna meet and talk things over. Is that so wrong? It's not like we're gonna meet and jump right in the sack."

"You sure about that?"

I looked away from the table and stared at a couple sitting across from us. They were holding hands and gazing into each other's eyes while chatting. In the background, the song "Secret Lovers" by Atlantic Starr began to play. I couldn't help wondering if they were secret lovers.

"Man, I said we're gonna talk."

Marc shook his head and raised a skeptical eyebrow. "Dave, I'm your boy, right?"

"Yeah."

"Then, as your boy, I'm gonna give you some advice. It may not be the advice you wanna hear, but I think it's advice you need to take." He paused and stared at me.

"What, man?"

"I don't agree with what you're doing, but if, and I do stress *if,* you do hook up with Jocelyn, you should forget about the love shit and just smash it for old-time's sake and then head straight back to Janelle."

"Come on, man," I said, frowning.

"Come on, man, nothing. Bruh, you don't want to fuck with a married woman. If you have to see her—fine—see her. But just do a 'wham, bam, thank you, ma'am,' and move on."

I shook my head. "Sorry, man, but Jocelyn means too much to me to do something like that. I can't and won't disrespect her like that."

"Bruh . . ."

"Give it a rest, Marc. This is about happiness. Happiness that I think I can have with Jocelyn. Hopefully our meeting will happen. Shit, it has to happen. I don't think I'll be able to move forward in any direction until it does."

"Damn, Dave. Like Usher said, 'You got it bad.' " I shrugged my shoulders, but didn't say anything.

Marc sighed. "All right, man, you win. You do what you feel you have to do. I got your back, whether I agree or not. Just do me a favor."

"What's that?"

"Tread wisely and remember this saying—be careful about throwing away some old ass for some new ass—well in your case, new older ass—because when you come back you might not have no ass."

We both laughed at his philosophical declaration.

"Anyway," Marc said, lifting his glass, "enough preaching. Lift your glass, playa, playa. I'm about to make a toast."

I lifted my glass. "A toast to what?"

"Here's to hope."

" 'Hope'?"

"Yeah. Here's to me hoping that you make the right decision. But if you don't, here's to hoping that you won't have to come by my place looking for an extra bed to lie in because you've been kicked out of your own. Smash it and run, bruh. *Salud.*"

We touched glasses together and downed the rest of our drinks. As we waited for our waiter, I thought to myself how glad I was that Janelle decided not to come along as originally planned. Even though Marc wasn't all for it, I was excited about the possibility of seeing Jocelyn again. I looked over at the couple again. They were still holding hands. Maybe they weren't secret lovers. Maybe it was the second time around for them.

Jocelyn

Crazy.

That's what I must have been.

It was one o'clock in the morning and I had just finished reading David's response to my e-mail. He was engaged. *Now what?* We were both involved, but we both wanted to see each other again. I couldn't believe this was happening. *After all this time*, I thought. Never in a million years did I ever think I'd be entertaining the thought of being with David again. When he cheated on me years back, he truly broke my heart. I'd given all of myself to him, and I trusted him completely. When I walked in on him having sex with Theresa Cueves—a girl I hated and still hate—I was devastated. I never expected him to be unfaithful to me. He was always so different from every other guy. The way he carried himself, the way he talked, walked, dressed, kissed; David was special, and made me feel special. Breaking up was hard to do because I'd loved him so much, but there was no way I was going to stay with him after that.

I hated him for years after that. Just the mere mention of his name, whether it was about him or not, pissed me off. I ripped up every picture, letter, and threw away every memento that he'd ever given me. Eventually, as time passed, I was able to put the pain of betrayal behind me and move on.

And now six years later . . .

I sighed and looked down at my laptop. His e-mail was still on the screen. I let my eyes run over the words one more time.

Jocelyn,

How are you? I was glad to hear from you. I wasn't sure if you were going to write me back after the things I'd said. I know, after the e-mails we'd been exchanging, that was the last thing you were expecting to read. But it was true. I'm still in love in with you. Honestly, I've never stopped loving you. I wish I would have never screwed up the way I did. If I hadn't, maybe I'd be the one you'd be married to. That caught me by surprise. I won't lie. I had to pause after I read that part. You're married. I wish it weren't true. I guess I should say congratulations. Your husband's a lucky man—even if he doesn't know it.

Anyway, about your suggestion: I would love to meet with you again. Marc thinks I'm crazy. He says that I should let go of any hopes of being with you again because you're married. I know he's right with what he says, and he's just looking out for me, but I'll be real—it's hard to give up on being with you—especially knowing that you are unhappy. If there's one thing that you deserve, it's happiness. And just knowing that you want to meet with me again gives me all the confidence I need to know that I can bring that happiness to you. I know you're confused about what you feel, and I respect that. Maybe us meeting will help you sort through that confusion and help you decide what road you'd like to take. I won't lie . . . for right or wrong, I hope you choose the path toward me.

Anyway, before I get going, I guess I need to answer your question. Yes, I am involved with someone. Actually, I'm en-

gaged. Her name is Janelle. I'll understand if you decide not to go through with us meeting. But if you do decide to meet, maybe we can meet again this coming weekend if you're free. My schedule is clear if you can. Let me know.

Love Always,
David

He was engaged. I was married. We both wanted to meet. I closed my eyes for a couple of seconds and saw David smiling behind my lids. He was engaged. I was married. We both wanted to meet. I thought that to myself over and over before moving to the laptop to let him know that the coming weekend would be fine.

Marisol

I stared at my younger sister as she fidgeted with a wrinkle in her slacks. I knew that if she couldn't keep her hands still then something was on her mind, because Jocelyn is not one to stress over those kinds of things. Although she dresses stylishly for work, my sister, in my opinion, is too low-maintenance. She's an every day, all-day jeans-and-sweatshirt type of person. I think she does herself a disservice by dressing down so much. I'm not saying that she should be profiling all the time, but once in a while outside of work wouldn't hurt.

Me, I didn't believe in sweats, jeans or T-shirts. I wore only designer clothing. I liked to look good all the time. Appearance was everything in my book. Besides, I liked to make sure that my shit was correct, just in case I bumped into a fine-looking man.

I had my ex to thank for my off-the-hook wardrobe. We were married for ten years and as a VP for an advertising company, he was nice enough to give me half of his savings. Actually, the judge gave it to me. I guess she agreed that saying "I do" didn't mean that I'd also agreed to be his punching bag. I thought of my ex every time I shopped. Blu Cantrell said it best when she said, "Hit 'em up style." *You go,* chica.

I watched Jocelyn continue to mess with her pants like a child who'd done something wrong. Older than her by three years, I was pretty much the mother we never had.

Growing up, we were last on our mother's short list of priorities. Men, partying and shopping for herself—those were the things our mother seemed to care about, and not necessarily in that order. Jocelyn and I fit in somewhere after all of that. And eventually when she found a man with just enough money to suit her needs, we pretty much became non-existent.

I'd always been grown for my age, and because we never knew our father, Jocelyn grew up relying on me for discipline and guidance. Because of the way we came up, our bond was stronger than any two sisters could have.

"Jocelyn, tell me what's wrong."

"Mari," Jocelyn said with raised eyebrows, "why do you think something is wrong?"

"Oh, come on. I'm not stupid. I know you like I know the back of my hand. You have something on your mind, so spill it and stop playing with your clothes."

She fidgeted for a few seconds longer with the wrinkle in her slacks, which wasn't a wrinkle at all, but a crease. "Okay, okay. *Pero no puedes decir nada.* Just listen and hear me out."

"Okay. My lips are sealed for now," I said with a smirk. "But this better be good."

"Oh, it'll be something."

"Mmm hmm."

Jocelyn stood up and began to pace my living room. "Do you remember David Cray?"

I thought for a second. "Yeah, I remember David. What about him?"

She didn't answer right away and continued pacing around

my living room, occasionally stopping to look at old photographs of us together.

"Jocelyn," I called out, *"por favor.* Come here and talk to me." *I hate it when she stalls.*

"Jesus, Mari, I was just admiring your things."

"No, you were stalling."

Jocelyn flopped down on the couch. "Okay. Like I was saying, David . . . Well, it's been a while since we've spoken. Six years to be exact."

"Right, and in that time, you've gotten married, and your career has taken off. How is Eric anyway? Last time we spoke, he was about to become a partner in the law firm."

"Eric's fine, but I don't really want to talk about him or the law firm, okay?"

I shrugged my shoulders. If she didn't want to talk about her fine husband that was her choice. "Fine. I didn't realize it would bother you."

Jocelyn cleared her throat. "Thank you. Anyway, a few weeks ago, when I was in Philly, I bumped into him."

"Oh really?"

"Yes."

"And what happened?"

"I said hi."

"And then what?" I had a feeling this was going in a bad direction.

"He said hi back."

"Okay, so where are you going with this?" I asked impatiently.

"Well, we spoke for a while and talked about how we were doing. He's an author, you know. I've never told you, but I've read both of his books. He lives in New York now."

I looked at my sister. "Jocelyn, why are you telling me all of this?"

Jocelyn took a deep breath. "Okay, okay. Before we went our separate ways we exchanged e-mail addresses."

"And?" I said, knowing without a doubt this was not a good thing.

"And we started sending each other messages."

"Okay. Are you going somewhere with all of this?"

"He sent me a message."

I raised an eyebrow. "A message saying what?"

"He said some things. Things that really made me think."

"Like?"

"Like some feelings that he's had and still has for me. It was a pretty deep e-mail."

I sucked my teeth and shrugged my shoulders. "So he still loves you. Big deal. You're married."

"Well, the thing is I replied back to him, and . . ."

"And what?" I said, sitting forward.

Jocelyn hesitated for a second and then said, "And I said some things too."

"Oh no," I said, sitting back in the couch. "Please don't tell me any more."

"Mari, I've never gotten over David. Even before I saw him, I'd thought about him off and on. And now since I've seen him, I can't stop thinking about him."

"Jocelyn, old feelings always come up from time to time."

"It's not just old feelings, Mari. On my wedding day, do you remember how much I was crying? Well, I wasn't crying because I was happy. I cried because the night before, I dreamt I was marrying David. I always wanted to marry David. And even though he hurt me, it still hurt to marry someone other than him."

"But you were a kid then, Jocelyn. You were only twenty-one years old when you broke up with him. You had been with him since high school, and he was all you knew. Shit, he was your first. Forget crying and forget David. You have a real man in Eric, who is good to you and good for you."

"Sí, Mari. Eric is good to me. But I don't feel for him what

I felt for David . . . what I *still* feel for David. Eric loves his job, but he doesn't love me. Not the way I need to be loved."

"Jocelyn, *hermanita,* how can you be so sure?"

"I just am. I know in my heart that David might be the one. That's why I've agreed to meet him this weekend."

"What?" I yelled out. "What do you mean you've agreed to meet him?"

"I just want to see if I'm right about what I feel."

"You're insane, *hermanita.*"

"No, I'm not. For whatever reason, David and I bumped into each other and the spark is still there. I want you to help me prove it."

"What do you mean you want me to help you?"

"I want you to help me come up with a way for our meeting to happen without making Eric suspicious."

"Oh, you have definitely lost your damn mind. You want me to help you cheat on your husband? Come on! There's no way in hell I'm helping you do that."

"Mari, *por favor. Tu eres mi hermana. Mi familia.* Besides, I am not cheating on Eric. This is just a meeting between old friends."

"Yeah—who used to be old lovers. Tell me something . . . Is he married? Because you certainly are."

Jocelyn quickly rose from her seat and approached me with puppy eyes. When we were kids and she needed me to do something sneaky for her, she would always come to me and look at me with those eyes. Damn her for that, because she knew that I could never say no when she did that. But this time I would be strong.

I looked away. "Don't even try to give me those eyes, Jocelyn, because it's not happening. I am not helping you sneak around on your husband. No way, no how."

Jocelyn gently placed her hands on my broad shoulders. "Mari, *mírame, por favor.*"

I shook my head in defiance. I wasn't giving in.

"Mari, look at me," Jocelyn insisted again.

I shook my head again, but as I did, my neck started to turn. "I'm not doing it," I said weakly, as my backbone started to disappear. "No way." And then I looked right into her damn puppy eyes.

"Mari, you know I wouldn't ask you to help me if I didn't believe in this."

"But, Jocelyn, is he married?"

"No. He's engaged."

"Jocelyn!" I tried to push her hands off of me, but she held firm.

"Mari, please help me. At least give me the opportunity to see if I am right. I need this chance."

"No. What you need is to stop thinking crazy. David's engaged, you're married and this is the first time you've seen him in six years. Can you see the sense I'm making? I mean, do I need to spell it out any clearer?"

"Mari, please? This is something that I need to do. Please don't make me do this without you."

Jocelyn stared at me with intent in her pleading eyes. I had never known anyone more determined than her. No matter what it was, if she wanted it, she would get it. I could always tell by her eyes when she was determined to make something happen regardless of the consequences. And I could tell then, by her unflinching stare, that she was going to make her meeting with David happen with or without my help. I couldn't help but envy her tenacity. It was something I never had.

I shook my head. "Jocelyn, for being so tiny, you have the biggest balls out of anyone I've ever known."

"I know. And you love me for it. So will you help me?"

"Jocelyn, this isn't right."

"This is right, Mari. I know it. I can't explain it, but I can feel it."

"What about Eric? Have you even thought of the consequences? There are all kinds of things to take into consideration . . . like your marriage."

Jocelyn breathed in deeply as she stood up. I had to play devil's advocate for her. After she and David ended their relationship, she had a string of unsuccessful, meaningless relationships. Men seemed to care less for her personality and more for her body. I wish I had that trouble. I remember when she declared that men were only capable of one-liners and attempts at one-night stands, and that she was giving up on all men.

Then she met Eric.

"He was in the bookstore looking at books in the financing section," she told me. "It just so happened that I went out that night to purchase the very same book he was browsing through. We spoke for a while in the store and then continued our conversation over dinner. Mari, I was so fascinated by his intelligence and the fact that he didn't stare at my breasts."

"He must have had a problem with his eyes that day," I joked.

They dated for a while and got married a year later. I was happy for her.

At the time, Eric was a welcome addition to her lonely and unfulfilled life. He was caring, sensitive, and career-driven. But his drive for success put distance between them.

"He's working late again. That's all he does," Jocelyn complained over and over again to me.

Those late nights inevitably turned into late weeks and late weekends. Anybody could see that his hours were taking its toll on their relationship.

Little by little, she began to resent his work ethic. I admit, it even started to bother me. Especially after the night I called her to congratulate them on their anniversary.

"At least you remembered." Jocelyn was in tears.

"You mean he forgot?"

"About the only thing he remembers to do now is brush his teeth and go to work."

I let her curse and vent for a few and then hung up the phone. It was a week before Eric remembered the anniversary.

Despite the problems they were having, I still wanted my sister to consider all that she wanted to do.

"I don't want to think about Eric right now," she said, turning her back to me.

"You have to think about Eric, Jocelyn. Just because you guys have been having problems—"

"Eric doesn't call them problems. He says we just have different views about our relationship. He is fine with the way things are going, and I think it's going nowhere."

I rose from the couch and stood beside her.

For a few minutes we stood in silence and stared outside at the squirrels gathering nuts for storage. Autumn was our favorite time of the year. As kids growing up, we enjoyed raking leaves into piles then jumping into the middle of them. Our pleasure was doubled when our mother would yell at us for walking into the house with flakes of the dried leaves clinging to our clothing and hair. Anything we could do to upset our mother, we made sure to do, to try and win her attention.

Once, we even went so far as to run away to a friend's house for an entire week. We were looking forward to hearing our friend's phone ring with a call from our mother, looking for us. That's what's supposed to happen, right? Kids disappear and their parents call all of their friends. Wrong. That call never came. Not there or anywhere else. Our mother never even noticed that we were gone. When we went home, her only concern was that we didn't disturb her and her new "friend."

Neither Jocelyn nor myself had spoken to her in over five years. She only tried to contact us once as adults, because she knew we both had money. In some not-so-nice words, we told her not to call again. She hadn't since.

"You ever think about Mom?" I asked.

Jocelyn sucked her teeth. "What for? She doesn't think about us. What made you ask me that anyway?"

I shrugged my shoulders. "I don't know. I guess us standing here, looking out at the leaves. It made me think of Mom, of the attention she never used to give us. It was hurtful, wasn't it?"

Jocelyn shrugged but didn't say anything.

"You could almost say Eric's doing the same thing, huh?"

Again she shrugged. Even though she hadn't responded, it was kind of obvious that our mother's lack of attention only made Eric's neglect hurt that much more.

"So when did you start thinking about David?"

Jocelyn continued to stare outside. "I guess more and more as I became unhappier. Over this past year especially, I would just wonder every now and then how he was and what he was doing. I almost tried to contact him once. That's why it's so crazy that we bumped into each other."

I laid my arm around her shoulder. "This is crazy, you know. Even if you guys had some sort of chemistry again, he lives in New York and you live in Maryland. How do you expect it to work?"

"I don't know yet. I just want to take it one step at a time. But I know I need to take this first step."

I looked at her. I could see the tension behind her hazel eyes. I could also see the excitement—a glow that I hadn't seen in a while. "I'm not sure about this. Why not try to fix what's broken with Eric?"

"Please." She stared at me with those puppy eyes again.

"Damn it, stop looking at me! Okay, okay, if you want to take this chance, then I guess I'll take it with you. But we need to talk about what has to happen and how. If you're going to do this, you better do it right."

"Thank you, Marisol."

"Yeah, yeah. I'll let you explain, when they're trying to keep me from getting into heaven."

Eric

While my wife slept peacefully beside me, I lay on my side and lightly caressed her cheek. I was a lucky man, and I knew it. I had a life-mate who was not only successful, intelligent and caring, she was beautiful too. But something was wrong, and had been for a long time. Lately there was a difference about her. A change in her behavior and in the way she moved. I'm sure to everyone else she seemed normal, but no one else knew her like I did. I was worried. I was already well aware of her frustrations over my job. I too had become exasperated.

Success wasn't an easy thing to attain, especially when you're a black lawyer in a white firm where the partners would rather have you serve them water than drink alongside them. If my father hadn't gone to school with Jim Kochner, the lead partner of the firm, I probably never would have been hired. Working for Kochner, Pine, and Schultz was oftentimes frustrating. Excluding Jim, there was a lot of hidden racism that I had put up with on a day-to-day basis. If theirs wasn't the biggest and most successful firm to work for, I would have quit and taken my determination and skill elsewhere. But instead of stepping out of the fire, I chose to stay in by setting a personal goal of becoming the first black partner with the firm. And as hard as that might have been, I was determined to make it happen.

My drive for success had a lot to do with my father, who was also a lawyer. When I was a kid growing up, it almost seemed like my father had my life and career pre-planned. With little input from me, he decided what college I would go to—John Jay College in New York—his alma mater, and what courses I would study. He even knew what type of law I would practice—criminal law.

I worked my butt off in college, doing whatever it took to succeed, because I didn't want to disappoint my father. I was happy with what I'd achieved, but for my Dad, it wasn't enough. By becoming a partner I was hopeful that I may have actually gotten one step closer toward hearing him tell me that he was proud of me.

Unfortunately, my desire to make my father proud had driven a wedge between Jocelyn and me. I didn't like the distance that all of the work had created, but working more than everyone else was what I had to do. I had to be the best. I tried to ignore my conflict with Jocelyn, but I knew that as each moment passed, I lost her just a little bit more.

I slowly leaned forward and kissed her forehead. She stirred and turned on her side, leaving me to look at her back. I whispered, "I love you," and lay back down.

Somehow, I had to make it up to her. I had to show her just how much she meant to me. There was no way I could let our love go anymore than it already had. I'd never told her, but there was a joy I got when I woke up and the first thing I saw was her angelic face. Maybe I should have told her that. Maybe she needed to hear these things from me. I had to do something. Something to show her how serious I was about her. About us. About our future. I knew just the thing. Some-thing that we'd talked about in the past. Yeah. I closed my eyes and fell asleep with a smile, knowing that I was going to make everything all right.

Marc

"I need a favor, man."

I looked over at Dave. I had a feeling I wasn't gonna like what the favor was. "What's up?" I asked, sucking in air.

Dave looked back at me and then wiped sweat from his own forehead. "You're my boy, right?"

"Yeah."

"I mean we're practically brothers, right?"

"Just spill it, bruh."

"I need you to cover for me this weekend."

I stopped pedaling. "What do you mean you need me to cover for you? Dave . . . come on, bruh. You're not really gonna hook up with Jocelyn, are you?" I looked at him with a disapproving eye. Even though he hadn't budged after our last conversation, I was still hoping by some miracle that he'd give up on trying to meet with Jocelyn. "She's married, man," I reminded him again for the umpteenth time.

Dave sighed. "I know, Marc."

"You did tell her about Janelle, right? Man, I told you that you can't keep her a secret." I got off the bike. I was really disappointed in him. I wasn't trying to be in love, but if I was and I had the right woman at my side, I wouldn't have been trying to screw it up like he was. I shook my head and walked off, headed toward the locker room.

"Yo, I told her," Dave said, coming beside me.

I turned around. "What?"

"I said I told her. She knows about Janelle."

"And she still wants to hook up with you?" I couldn't believe it. I was almost positive that she'd back off when he told her.

"Yeah, man."

"Damn," was all I could say. I started to walk again.

"We're gonna hook up this coming weekend. And I could use your help in making that happen."

"My help?"

"Yeah. I'm gonna tell Janelle that I have to do something with you this weekend. I don't know what yet, but I'll think of something. I just need for you to have my back and cover for me in case she calls your cell."

"Dave, man, you need to think about what you're doing," I said as we walked into the locker room. "You have a lot to lose." I tossed my bag on the bench between the lockers and peeled off my soaked tank top.

"I know what I have to lose," Dave said, unlocking his locker. "You don't have to remind me."

"So if you know, why are you doing this?

"Because, man, I have a lot to gain too. I told you, man . . . this could be it for me."

I watched Dave with a serious eye as I undressed. I wanted to protest some more, but I could tell by the way he stared back at me that his mind was made up. With or without me, he was going through with this.

I sighed. "I hope you know what you're doing, bruh."

Dave nodded. "So you gonna cover for me or what?"

"Man, you don't even have to ask."

Dave put out his hand and smiled. "Good lookin' out, man."

"Yeah, yeah," I said, wrapping a towel around my waist.

Dave laughed and then looked at the towel. "Yo, you never shower at the gym. What's up?"

I smiled. "Man, I got a date."

"'A date'?"

"Yeah, bruh. I hooked up with this fine Trinidadian sister at work."

Dave zipped up his bag and stood up. "So when did you hire this one?"

"Three weeks ago."

"Three weeks? Why so long? You usually snatch them up within the first week."

"Man, I was busy with other honeys. Kid, she is banging! Her body had to be shaped from heaven because she's got curves I didn't know existed." I took off my sweats and boxers and wrapped the towel around my waist. "And check it, her name is Dahlia. Trust me, brotherman, I'm looking to be her Sampson." I laughed.

"That's *Delilah*, fool. And when are you gonna stop going for only the women you hire?"

"Why would I want to do that? The females I bring on are top-notch. They're young, they're fit, and they're fine. What more could I ask for?"

"How about something besides sex, Don Juan?"

"Sheeeit," I said, making my way toward the showers. I hated showering with other guys around. I was scared they'd start staring at the package I had. But I had to pick Dahlia up right after the gym. "What else is there? I'll leave the sappy shit to you fools. Call me later, and we'll talk more about this weekend."

"Will do."

As Dave walked out of the locker-room, I was singing

loudly in the showers, "Why do fools fall in love?" With water spraying down over my head, I smiled to myself.

I was looking forward to the date. I know I made it seem like it was all about the sex, but the truth was I was feeling Dahlia like I'd never felt any other female. She had a quick wit and sharp tongue, which I loved. She was intelligent as hell and best of all, unlike every other female I'd messed with, when she came in for the interview it was all about the job for her. She didn't sweat me in any way at all. That's what got me.

I lied when I told Dave I'd hired her three weeks ago. The real truth was she'd actually been working for me well over two months. Of course I tried to spit game after she started, but no matter what I said or did, no matter how many times I flashed my smile and licked my lips, Dahlia never paid any attention to me. She let me know "from the gate" that she was there to work and because she did, I was forced to do something I'd never done before—give up the flirting. With her, of course. So instead of treating her like a piece of fine ass, I treated her like an employee who could help my business prosper. I guess she liked the new approach I'd taken because a couple of weeks after that, she actually asked me out. This too was something I would've never, ever admitted to Dave or anyone else.

My feelings for Dahlia was one of the main reasons I had really given Dave a hard time about messing with Jocelyn. I could understand his desire to see her, because of the way I was feeling Dahlia, but I just didn't want him to lose the good thing he had with Janelle. Plus, I was worried about him fucking with a married woman. *Oh well,* I thought as I turned to stream massage my back. It was on him. I knew what I wanted.

I smiled and thought about Dahlia. "Damn, I can't believe this bug is hitting me," I said out loud.

To my right, an older black gentleman with a barrel of a

stomach looked at me and smiled. "Drink a lot of orange juice, young buck. Vitamin C. It'll flush that bug right out of you."

"You think so?"

The old man turned off his shower and grabbed his towel. "I know you're big and strong, young buck, but take it from an old man. Drink the orange juice and take some vitamins. That bug will be gone in no time."

I smiled to myself as he walked away. "Orange juice," I said. When I got home, I planned on emptying whatever orange juice I had left. For the first time ever, I had no intention of letting the bug get away.

Jocelyn

"I was awake when Eric touched me, but I kept my back to him. Mari, it was so hard to keep the tears from falling."

"Jocelyn, he cares more than you know."

"It's been so long since he has done anything like that. He even whispered that he loved me."

"He does. Maybe he's going to start trying harder."

"But it almost feels like it's too late."

"'Too late'? How can it be?"

"But, David . . ."

"But, David, nothing. You haven't met David yet. You don't have to meet him."

"Mari, we talked about this before. My mind and heart is made up. There is no changing my mind on this."

"But—"

"No buts, okay? Eric had his chance, and now I want to take mine."

"Your chance at what? Losing real love over a fantasy?"

"Mari, this isn't a fantasy. This is real love. I know it."

"How can you, Jocelyn? People change. You and David had six years to change."

"Mari, I just know, okay. Look, I have to go. I'll talk to you later."

I hung up the phone, closed my eyes and sighed. As much as I loved my sister and valued her advice, I couldn't give in to what she was saying. In the darkness behind my eyelids I saw David. And when Eric had touched my cheek, it was David's hand that I felt.

Despite the guilt that danced on the edge of my soul, I was falling fast and hard for David and for a freedom that I hadn't known for a long time. Mari's advice was sound advice, and any other time I would have really given her words heavy consideration. But I couldn't this time, because she had no clue what I was feeling inside, not only for David, but Eric as well.

When I got home, I was exhausted. All day at work, my thoughts kept drifting back to David. I reminisced about the past and kept daydreaming about our meeting this coming weekend. To be honest, other than my fantasizing, I didn't really remember what else I did at work. I had a couple of meetings; I remembered that much because my notepad was lined with red and black ink, with asterisks beside a few sentences.

Since Eric wasn't going to be home, my plan was to turn on a pot of coffee, put on a few CDs, and go back over my notes and e-mails from the day. So when I opened the front door, I was caught completely off guard by what lay before me.

Lined along the floor in the hallway were cinnamon-scented candles and in the middle of the hallway, hanging from the ceiling by a thin piece of thread, was a single red rose with a piece of paper taped to it. For a brief moment I actually wondered if I had accidentally walked into the wrong house, but of course, I couldn't have because my keys had worked in the lock.

Curiously and cautiously, I stepped inside, approached the rose, removed the slip of paper, and read what was written:

A single rose for the lone woman in my life—walk forward.

Confusion was running through my mind as I pulled the rose from the string. *What the hell is Eric up to?* I continued forward, and when I stepped into the living room, I was once again taken back as I stared at a group of candles set in rows on each side of the room, to resemble pews in a church. The expensive leather sofas and oak coffee table were nowhere to be seen. Lining the rows, protruding from red vases, were more roses.

I walked down the candle-made aisle to the dining area. Sitting in the middle of the aisle was another vase with one rose and another note attached. I removed the note:

The roses on the side represent others who are looking in from the outside.
They are envious of our love.
This rose, combined with the other, completes the bond between us.
This bond is unbreakable and was sealed by love—walk forward.

My heart was beating heavily at this point, and my hands were damp with perspiration. I slowly moved forward, and for the first time, I realized that my favorite Natalie Cole CD was playing from the stereo. What was Eric doing home? What was the reason behind the romance? As bad as it sounds, I had actually been looking forward to another night of loneliness.

I couldn't hide my frown, when Eric appeared from the kitchen, dressed in a tuxedo. I didn't say anything right away. I just stared at him with bewildered eyes as he looked back at me with a slight grin. In his hand, he held three more roses. I didn't speak until he came forward, handed the roses to me, and took my hand.

"What are these roses for?"

He put his finger to my lips. "Shhh. I'll tell you, but first you have to sit down." He led me to the dining table, pulled back a chair, took my coat and laptop, and allowed me to sit. The table itself was no less spectacular than the aisle or the hallway. Candles sat in the middle, and a bottle of champagne rested in a bucket of ice to the side. The table had been set with the china given to us on our wedding day—china that we rarely used.

As Eric gathered the plates to fill them with food, I laid the roses on the table and took a deep breath.

I hadn't been treated this way in such a long time. It was so romantic and so carefully thought out. It was everything that I had once been accustomed to. But as time went by, Eric had become less attentive and too busy to do things like that anymore. Our life together had become so routine that, as I exhaled slowly, I realized just how numb I had become to his attempt at rekindling the flame.

He came back with a plate full of rice and green peas, with steak smothered in gravy, and mashed potatoes on the side. "I hope you enjoy it."

Before sitting down, he grabbed the champagne bottle and popped the cork. After pouring some into two glasses, he handed me one and took his own. "This is a toast to you," he said softly. "You are my life, and I just wanted to let you know that." He touched my glass with his and swallowed his drink down.

When he noticed that I hadn't touched my glass he asked, "Are you okay?"

I looked down and sighed. Somewhere deep inside, I felt myself becoming angry. *Too little, too late* was all I was thinking. "I'm all right. I'm just not in the mood for alcohol right now." I set the glass down on the table and massaged my temples. "I have a headache and I had a rough day today."

"Okay."

I could hear the disappointment in his voice. I could also feel tension building in the cinnamon-scented air.

"Well, try to eat. Maybe it will help."

"I'm sorry, Eric, but I'm not really hungry. I appreciate all of this. You just caught me on a lousy day."

Eric's brows furrowed, and I could see his hands trembling slightly as he held his fork in his hand. "Couldn't you at least try to have a few bites? I took the day off today to set everything up. I even slaved over the stove to make this. And you know the kitchen and I don't get along."

"Maybe later I'll try. Right now I just want to lie down." I slowly began to push away from the table, when he grabbed my hand.

"Jocelyn, let's start a family."

I looked up at him. "What?"

"A family—let's do it. Let's start one. We're both financially stable, and we're both still young. Let's do it while the time is right."

I looked at him and if he couldn't see it before, I was sure he could see the confusion in my eyes now. "Eric, what the hell are you thinking? We can't start a family now."

He held up his hand in protest. "Listen, I know that things haven't been the same between us for a while now, and I know that a large portion of that is because of me. I've been putting so many hours into work that I've been neglectful at home. I don't blame you for being apprehensive about this. But, believe me, I love you and want nothing more than to raise a family with you. We're not so far along in our hole that we can't climb out of it." He held on to my hand firmly, despite my attempt to pull away. "That's why I have three roses. The three equal a family. Please. This is something we've both talked about."

"That was in the past, Eric. Things were different then."

"We can make it like it was. I'm willing to put the time and effort in."

" 'Time and effort'? What are you going to do, Eric—add me to your schedule?" I was getting warm with anger as I stared at him. His sudden re-emergence with love and affection was the last thing I had expected or wanted.

I pulled my hand away and stared at him without saying a word. I tried, but I couldn't keep my angry tears from running over. He looked back at me with confusion. I knew he didn't expect that type of reaction from me. Didn't he understand how far into that hole we had already gone?

"Jocelyn . . . I love you. I just want us to be happy. I want us to be a family. A real family."

"Damn it, Eric!" I suddenly yelled. "Goddamn it. How can you ask this of me now? What do you expect me to do? Jump into your arms and say, 'Yes, let's do it! Let's have a fucking baby!' Do you realize that for this entire month, we have eaten dinner together only three times? Three, damn it! You spend more time with your job than you do with me. Do you know that? Did you really expect me to fall head over heels with what you've done tonight? Are you really that blind?"

"I . . . I know things have been different. But I just felt—"

" 'Felt'?" I screamed out. I was past anger at this point; I felt nothing but resentment. "You want to know what I felt, Eric? I felt you were happier fucking your job than your own wife."

"Come on, Jocelyn, don't be ridiculous."

I slammed my fist on the table and stood up. *'Ridiculous'*? He had the nerve to call me ridiculous! My glass of champagne fell over and spilled onto our cream-colored carpeting. "Ridiculous? *Maldita sea!* The only thing that's ridiculous is your suggestion about us having a baby. We barely have a marriage and you say, 'Let's have a baby!' When did you realize you actually had a wife and not a roommate?"

This time, Eric stood up. His glass also fell over, though it was empty. "I have never treated you like a roommate. I have always—am always there. How can you say these things to me? I'm not a perfect man, you know. I work hard to put food on the table."

"For what? So that you can eat by yourself? And let's not forget, I work just as hard to put that food there too."

"I wasn't implying that you didn't. Come on, Jocelyn." He moved toward me but stopped abruptly as I backed away.

I didn't want him to touch me.

He stared at me in quiet disbelief.

I knew that he had planned the evening out thoroughly. Everything was supposed to go so differently. I was sure he had envisioned a night of conversation and laughter, and if he was lucky, topped off by ravenous lovemaking.

He laid his hands against his waist and lowered his head. I watched him the whole time and damned myself silently at the same time.

The problems we were having weren't entirely his fault. Especially since David had come back into my life. Anger and guilt were beating me down. I had to get out of there.

Without saying another word, I turned and went upstairs to grab some clothing to take with me. I decided to go by Marisol's to calm down and clear my head.

When I finished packing, I paused at the top of the staircase to brace myself for round two with Eric. I didn't think he was going to let me go without a fight, especially when he saw my bags. But to my surprise, he didn't say a word to me and with him standing silent and stoic, I grabbed my keys and headed toward the door. I never looked back as I walked out of our home.

In my car, I sat behind the wheel and wiped tears of frustration away from my eyes. My keys were in the ignition, but it wasn't turned on. I wasn't in a rush to get to Mari's. I didn't really want to be around her or anyone at that particular moment. My head was hurting with all kinds of emotions—guilt, resentment, relief.

I inhaled and exhaled, and lightly touched my laptop case. I hadn't even realized that I had grabbed it on the way out. I stared at it and knew instantly the one person I could talk to. The one person who would understand what I was going through.

Eric

I was drunk as I sat alone and drank straight from the bottle of champagne I had purchased for my romantic evening gone to hell. I listened to the clamor of silence and shook my head. I wasn't supposed to be alone with pain and heartbreak sitting by my sides, keeping me company. In my mind, the scene had played out much differently. The noises were supposed to have been louder, happier, and eventually lust-filled. And then within the year to come, baby sounds were supposed to become part of the equation. I was ready for that, and I had mistakenly assumed that Jocelyn was too. I took another long swallow and sighed. I was unaccustomed to being on the losing end. In sports, I was always on the winning team. With girls, I always had the best-looking one. My success continued after high school, followed me throughout my collegiate career as a straight-A student, and endured into my professional career. All my life I had gotten what I wanted. That rule applied even with Jocelyn.

Of all places, we met in the bookstore. She was dressed in nothing more than a pair of sweats and a T-shirt, but I could not recall ever seeing a woman as naturally beautiful as she was. There was nothing made-up about her. I believe our meeting was fate, because the very book I was browsing through was the one she had come to buy—and it just happened to be the last one.

After introducing myself, we talked for a little while and then decided to go out for a bite to eat.

We were married a year later.

Now, with three wedding anniversaries behind us, I had doubts about there being a fourth.

I swallowed down the rest of the champagne then threw the bottle across the room and watched it shatter against the wall. Why the hell was I being punished for wanting to succeed? All my hard work, all of the time I'd put in—isn't that what I was supposed to do as a husband?

I tried her cell a few times, but she never answered. All I could do was grit my teeth and shake my head. I was taking care of business, being a good provider, yet I felt like I was the bad guy. How was that fair?

I tried her cell a few more times, and when she didn't answer, I left her a voice mail, telling her that I loved her and then went to bed.

David

David,

I can't stand it anymore. I'm sitting here at Barnes and Noble drinking a vanilla latte, trying to calm down. Things are just too damn frustrating for me at home. Eric wants to start a family. He hasn't paid me any attention in the past year and he wants to have a family? He was always so damn busy with work. Did he really expect me to say yes? He even had the nerve to say he was working to put food on the table—as if I don't bring money into the household. I'm sorry to vent this way. I guess I'm also a little confused because I know that I feel something very strong for you, but at the same time I am married. I know that nothing has happened yet, and nothing may happen. But what if it does? I wish wanting to see you didn't have to be so hard. I really hope that we are making the right decision. I don't want anyone getting hurt. But then I guess that's already happening, isn't it?

I admit, though, I am dying to see you. Why does this week have to go by so slowly? I've told Marisol that I will be meeting with you. She's against us meeting and has tried to talk me out if it, but I got her to agree to help me anyway. I can't blame her *for her skepticism, though. No one but you and I could possibly understand what we feel. I can't believe this is all happening. The weekend isn't coming fast enough for me. Let me know what time you will be coming on Friday. I have a room booked at the Hyatt in Baltimore at the harbor. It is room 614. We will have our privacy there. I just want to see you again. After that, whatever happens will happen. Only our hearts will know. Honestly, I want to feel your arms wrapped around me tightly again the way they used to be. I will be there waiting for you,* corazón.

Para Siempre,
Jocelyn

I closed the e-mail and sat back against my chair. Sade was whispering from the stereo. She was asking me if it was a crime that she still wanted me. No, it wasn't a crime at all. I could almost hear Jocelyn speaking the words from the e-mail to me. I could almost see her standing before me. Almost. But not yet. Not until Friday, which was two days away.

I had everything planned out with Marc. I'd tell Janelle at the last minute that Marc and I were going to see his parents and would be gone for the entire weekend. Telling her last minute like that was the one sure way to guarantee that she wouldn't be able to come because she wouldn't have enough time to get everything ready.

When Janelle traveled, she packed everything. Packing in fifteen minutes was definitely not her style.

I was ready. I would "accidentally" forget to take my cell phone so that she couldn't contact me, and neglect to leave Marc's parents' phone number. It had taken me seconds to formulate the plan, but somehow, I felt as if I had always been prepared. It was weird, but it was almost as if I knew this opportunity would come.

As I sat up and prepared to send a reply, Janelle walked into the living room and sat down beside me.

"David," she said quietly. She was draped in her bathrobe, with a towel wrapped around her head. "Can we talk for a minute?"

I quickly closed my e-mail. "I was just about to do some writing."

She gently placed her hand on mine. "Please? This is important."

I could hear the sincerity in her tone and see the seriousness in her eyes. I gently squeezed her hand and pushed my laptop to the side. "Okay, let's talk."

"Is there someone else?" Janelle asked without emotion.

I watched her as my heart beat heavily. Her gaze was unflinching. "What kind of question is that?"

"It's an honest one."

"'Honest'? What do you mean by that?"

"David, things are different between us. You're different."

I clenched my jaws and tried not to let the troubled look in her eyes get to me as I prepared to lie. "Look, Janelle, before we go any further, no, there isn't anyone else. Now I'll admit I've been a little distant lately, but I've been under a lot of pressure. I'm having some major problems with my new book, and my agent's pressuring me for a completed manuscript. But, Janelle, I'm not the only one who's been different. You haven't exactly been the same either." I hated to turn the table on her like that, but I had no choice.

Janelle nodded. "I know."

"Then why ask me if I'm cheating on you?"

"Look, I'm sorry, David. I'm just frustrated. I don't like for things to be the way they are between us."

"Neither do I," I said. I stood up and went to the stereo to shut it off. The CD had stopped playing, but I just needed to get away from the pained look on her face.

"Then let's do something about it. Let's change things. Let's find a way to fix what's breaking."

I looked at my woman as she sat with her fingers intertwined. Her shoulders were slumped, and her eyes were pleading for a resolution. I'd never felt more guilty about what I was doing than that particular moment. This woman loved me. I sighed. "Well, what do you suggest we do? What do you want from me?"

"David, it's not about what I want from you or what you want from me. It's about what we want. *We.* That's what's been missing. We're not a unit anymore. Look at the amount of time we spend together."

"We both work."

"That never used to matter. We used to spend hours working, but at the end of the day we always came together. We always had time for one another. Tell me, why has that changed? What the hell happened to us?"

I exhaled. "I don't know," I said bluntly.

"I don't either," she said, her voice dropping to a whisper.

I went around, sat beside her, and cupped my hand under her chin. The guilt I was feeling was making my stomach burn, but I couldn't turn back.

"Look, why don't we plan a trip together? We'll go to a place where it's just you and me. No work, no distractions. Just you, me and love. How does that sound?"

"I love you," she said, crying softly. "I'm really not trying to be a bitch or anything."

"I know. Stop crying, okay." I wrapped my arms around her and cursed myself for each and every word I'd said. I gently rocked her back and forth and ground my teeth.

The last thing I had ever intended to do was hurt her. But deep inside, I knew that pain would be unavoidable. I wiped the tears away from the corner of her eyes and kissed her softly on the lips. She kissed me back strongly, forcing her tongue into my mouth. I accepted her offering and stroked her tongue with my own.

As we kissed, she passed her hand over my crotch and moaned as I grew with excitement. Instinctively, I unfastened the belt of the robe she wore, exposing her breasts, and took one in my hand and caressed it.

She sighed and squeezed my erection, as I ran my tongue around her dark nipple. I guided my hands to the warmth between her legs and lightly touched the inside of her vagina. She opened her legs, allowing me to go farther inside. Her wetness made me throb even more.

"Let's go upstairs," she said in a whisper, running her hand up and down my shaft.

The weakling I was stood, and without a word, led her by the hand.

Janelle

After David and I made love, I lay in silence while he slept. This had become so damn routine for us. We talked about our problems and then made love, knowing that nothing would change. I wondered how long it would be before our next talk. I loved David with my entire being and didn't want to lose him, but it takes two to make things work, and I was getting tired of being the driver.

I gently nudged him in his side. "David," I said softly. "David, wake up."

He stirred and then opened his eyes. "What is it?" he said with a little bit of an edge, which surprised me.

I gave him a look to let him know I wasn't the one. "Why do we have to wait to go away? Why don't we go away this weekend?"

He moved away from beside me, sat up, and placed his feet on the floor.

"Did I say something wrong? Or have you changed your mind about wanting to make this work?"

"No, I haven't changed my mind. But we can't go this weekend."

"Why not?"

"I forgot to mention, but Marc asked me to go with him to his parents' place in Maryland."

"Why?"

"Marc's mom found his dad in bed with a twenty-three-year-old girl just out of college."

"Are you serious?"

"Yeah."

"That is so trifling. How could he do that to his wife?"

"I don't know, baby. But Marc wants to try and talk some sense into his father. And you know how hotheaded Marc can be. Just imagine the two of them going head-to-head in the same room. I'm going to be the mediator of sorts, see if maybe we can keep his parents together."

"Keep them together? Why would she want to stay with his cheating ass?"

"Baby, they've been married for over thirty-one years."

"Exactly. His ass had no right cheating on her now."

"Well, there's two sides to every story, Janelle. Maybe it wasn't all his fault. Maybe she drove him to be unfaithful."

I sat up in the bed. "So what are you saying? That she pushed him to cheat? That it's her fault he went and messed with some young skank?"

"Baby, I'm not saying that. I'm just saying that we need to hear both sides before we pass judgment. For whatever reason, he had an affair. Something made him do it."

I sucked my teeth. "I can't believe you are defending him like that. Something made him do it, my ass. Trifling. And in her bed, too."

David stood up from the bed. "Janelle, why are we even arguing about this? I don't know why he did what he did. He's human, and we all make mistakes. But is his mistake worth throwing away thirty-one years?"

I sucked my teeth again. "He should have thought of that before he unzipped his pants. I hope his mother is okay. I don't know why you men do that shit. You all want to be so dominant and so damn tough. Cheating is so cowardly. Why can't you ever come out and say you'd rather be with someone else? Make it easier on a woman. Marc's mom is such a beautiful woman, too. Why would he want to leave her for some fresh-out-the-water 'ho'?"

"You know the male ego. Maybe he's going through the whole mid-life crisis thing."

"Mid-life crisis, my ass. He's just some horny-ass man who can't keep his dick in his pants. Makes me sick. If you ever cheated on me . . . oooh. Anyway, maybe I can come and help, maybe offer some comfort for his mother. I'm sure she needs it."

David didn't answer me. He walked into the bathroom and turned on the cold water. I listened to him douse his face a few times and then I got up and walked into the bathroom behind him. He was staring at himself deeply into the mirror.

"Are you all right?"

He looked down into the sink and then looked into the mirror again. It almost seemed like he was gritting his teeth. Finally, he turned around, smiled and enveloped me in his arms. "Yeah, I'm fine. I just felt dizzy for a second."

"Are you sure you're okay?"

"Yeah. I'm just a little hungry, that's all. You wore me out."

I smiled. I did try to put it on him. "So anyway, what about my suggestion? You never answered me."

David squeezed me tightly. "Baby, you know I'd love for you to come with me, but under the circumstances, I think it'd be best if I went with Marc alone. This is a touchy situation. I think if you went it would only make his mom feel like everyone is up in her business, know what I mean?"

I sighed. My heart went out to her. "Yeah, I see what you mean. I'd probably feel that way too."

"It's a hard pill for her to swallow," he said, kissing my forehead. "I'm sure she would rather have as few people as possible know about the situation."

"You're probably right," I said, moving away from him. "Besides, leaving this weekend for anything would have been a bad idea anyway. I have a lot of work to do."

I left the bathroom and went back to the bedroom. When David stepped into the room, I noticed that he was sliding his feet into his slippers.

"You're not coming back to bed?"

"I'm going to grab a snack, and then I'm going to jump on the laptop for a few."

" 'The laptop'? You're going to write now?"

"Yeah. I just have that feeling, and I don't want to lose it."

"Can't you leave that laptop alone for a while and spend some time with me?"

"Baby, you know how I am about writing, when I have that feeling. I'll only be a few minutes. I promise."

I lay under the covers. "Whatever, David. You want to talk all this shit about making us work and you can't give up the feeling. Thanks for letting me know where your priorities are."

"Janelle, don't be like that. I said I'm only going to be gone for a few. I just want to get my thoughts down. I'll be back in bed before you know it."

"Whatever," I said coldly. I grabbed his pillow and threw it at him. "Why don't you just stay on the damn couch tonight, you and your laptop?" I buried my head under the covers, and when the bedroom door closed, I cried.

Jocelyn

It was Friday, and the longest week in my life had finally come to an end. I paced back and forth in the hotel suite I'd reserved for David and me, unable to keep still, and cursed myself for being too anxious and coming too early. I was a nervous wreck.

I sat down by the desk and tapped my fingers furiously on the wood. I took in a deep breath to try to calm myself and looked at my watch. It was only twelve o'clock. David wouldn't arrive until four or five. I stood up and started to pace again. Sitting still just seemed to make time slow down.

I picked up the remote control for the TV and flipped through the channels, in an attempt to pass some time, but it didn't work. I turned off the television and went to the window to stare down at the activity in the harbor below. The sun was out and shining brightly for everyone to enjoy. A reggae band played music while people danced, and others sat and listened from the different restaurants.

I sighed and stepped away from the hotel window and sat back on the bed. I hated waiting. I was never a very patient person. I looked around the room for the fifth time. I wanted everything to be perfect.

Before going to the hotel I stopped at a few stores to buy some necessary items for the weekend. My first stop was at Frederick's of Hollywood to purchase a couple of tantalizing outfits to make David's mouth water. It was all about seduction, when I bought peach-scented candles next. Eight, to be exact; four to be placed at each corner of the king-size bed with the satin sheets I laid out, and four for each corner of the bathtub/ Jacuzzi.

To add to the ambiance, I had several slow jam and jazz CD's programmed and ready for non-stop play. The icing on the cake was chilling in a bucket of ice in the miniature refrigerator by the mini-bar. Everything was ready, and all that I needed now was David.

I smiled as I daydreamed about how he and I would utilize the suite. I hadn't had this excited butterfly-in-the-pit-of-my-stomach feeling in a long time—since my first date with David, actually. Very few dates I'd had since then could measure up to that evening.

As though it were yesterday and not more than ten years ago, I still remember the romance.

David had taken me to a lake hidden by trees and tucked away behind a group of houses. It was mid-September, so it wasn't too hot. It was a perfect eighty-five-degree evening. The bright moon was full and bathing rays of moonlight over the subtle ripples that several ducks in the water created. David and I sat on a blanket near the water, talking and admiring the endless display of stars in the clear black sky.

Like that evening, David captivated me. I remember looking into his eyes as we spoke, thinking to myself how special he was and how safe I felt with him. We shared our first kiss that evening, and it was one that I had never forgotten, his full lips on mine, his gentle hands wrapped around my own.

"David," I whispered, lying back on the bed.

I moaned as my hands ran over the curves of my breasts.

"David," I whispered again.

Gone was the recollection of him and me at the lake. We were in the room now, naked on the bed with the candles aflame around us.

"David," I whispered, my hands traveling down to the now wet region between my thighs. I squirmed and gasped, as my fingers became David's and explored my femininity.

"Oh, David," I said once more, my body temperature rising, my ecstasy climbing higher and higher.

"David!" My legs spread wider, my back arched.

"David!" I yelled out as he pleasured my body in the way that he knew how. I climaxed powerfully as I sang out his name. I lay still and inhaled and exhaled deeply to help my heart rate slow down.

"David," I whispered once more. The time wasn't moving fast enough.

David

I forced myself to keep the car at a steady sixty-five miles per hour because I didn't want to get pulled over, not to avoid a speeding ticket, but not to be held back. After packing and saying good-bye to Janelle, I drove to Marc's house to finalize everything.

"Man, you sure you wanna go through with this?" he asked, looking at me.

I nodded. "I can't turn back. Not now."

Marc shrugged his shoulders. "Your call, man. I still can't believe you lied about my parents like that. Even worse, I can't believe Janelle fell for it. What kind of man does she think my pops is?"

Marc laughed, and I laughed with him.

"When she made the suggestion about coming, for a split second, I thought this weekend wasn't gonna happen. Luckily for me I was so convincing."

"Yeah, and now she thinks my pops is scum of the earth. Damn, man, I better make a trip to see my parents. I gotta make sure no shit like that is going down for real."

Marc's decision to visit his parents actually worked out

even better for me, because there was no way for Janelle to bump into him by accident. The way everything had fallen into place led me to think only one thing—this weekend was supposed to happen. Our meeting couldn't come quick enough.

I tightened my hand around the steering wheel and groaned as I was forced to drop from sixty-five to barely ten miles an hour. "Always when you're in a rush," I said, slamming my hand on the steering wheel.

I looked in the distance up ahead. I saw nothing but a line of cars all bumper to bumper. When three state troopers and two ambulances forced their way through the traffic twenty minutes later, I knew that I wasn't going anywhere any time soon.

I wondered what Jocelyn was doing at that moment. Was she as nervous and excited as I was? With this backup I hoped she didn't think that I wasn't going to make it. I pressed on my horn, just to vent.

Finally, about forty-five minutes later, the traffic began to move again. When I could finally press down on the gas pedal without having to worry about stopping, following the speed limit was not an option.

When I finally made it to the hotel, I parked the car in the garage and let out a long sigh of relief. My heart was beating heavily with anxious anticipation. I took a couple more deep breaths and then I rushed into the hotel.

As I waited for an elevator, I stood silent and thought about what was about to happen. I replayed different scenes over and over in my mind. Which one would make the final cut? I had no clue, but I was ready to find out. When the elevator arrived, I took one more hearty breath, and then stepped in and pressed the button for the sixth floor.

I stepped out of the elevator on the sixth floor and stood stock-still. I listened to the sounds within the hallway—televisions from behind closed doors, muted voices, and my own rhythmic heartbeat, which I heard above everything else. I took a few quick breaths and then approached a mirror directly across from the elevator to check my appearance. I was dressed in a black sweater with black dress slacks. I had on a black blazer to set off the entire ensemble. In my hands, I held a bouquet of red roses and a small box wrapped in silver paper with a red ribbon. My legs felt like they were made of rubber, and the palms of my hands were cold with perspiration. I looked at my watch, although I had checked it just two minutes prior. It showed six o'clock, much later than I had planned, but with the accident it had been unavoidable. But nevertheless I made it. I had never imagined that I would be as nervous as I was.

I smoothed my eyebrows then turned away from the glass and made my way toward room 614. My heart began to beat in triplets as I neared the room and thought about the actual moment when Jocelyn would open the door. What would we say or do? Hopefully I wouldn't stumble over my words. I passed room 610, and my heart dropped to my stomach. When I passed room 612, it rose, and my legs seemed to lock.

Finally, I stood before room 614. I stopped and listened to the hallway's sounds again. Perspiration trickled down the middle of my back, and for a quick second, I wondered if I had forgotten to put on deodorant. I checked quickly, just for good measure, and then reached up to knock on the door. That's when I noticed how unsteady my clenched hand was. I closed my eyes and breathed at a snail's pace, trying to steady the jittering. Then I knocked.

Jocelyn

My body shuddered when the knock on the door came. David. I rose from the bed slowly on wobbly legs. This was the moment I had been waiting for. This was the moment for which I had been willing to risk whatever happiness I currently had. I felt my body temperature rise, yet I still shivered. I shook my hands to calm the nerves that danced at the edges of my fingertips. Breathing in deeply, I smoothed the black gown that embraced my body. It was sleeveless and as I moved, my right leg peeked out from a thigh-high slit on the side. I felt sexier than I had in a long time.

I approached the door and felt the excitement tumble in the pit of my stomach. I smiled and touched my cheeks; I was sure they were flush. I hoped that David wouldn't notice.

I lay my hand on the doorknob and closed my eyes. For fear of seeming overanxious, I waited for another knock.

Another thirty seconds passed by, and then it came.

I closed my fingers around the brass knob, opened my eyes, and pulled the door open. A knot rose in my throat.

David stood in the doorway. "Hello, Jocelyn."

Unexpectedly, and before I could fight them back, tears

welled in my eyes and fell down across my cheeks. "David," I struggled to say.

He moved forward and gently took me in his arms, and as he held me, the tears fell harder, dampening his shirt.

"Jocelyn," he whispered. He squeezed me and kissed my forehead.

Any nervousness I may have previously felt was gone, replaced now by euphoria. Right then and there, I knew that whatever gamble I had taken had been worth it. I hadn't noticed them before, but he bent down and gently placed a bouquet of roses and a boxed gift on the ground beside him. Then he stood up and placed his finger beneath my dimpled chin and lifted my face toward his.

We stared at one another, and as we did, I remembered the many times we had done that in the past.

"Jocelyn," David said again. Then he rested his lips gently against mine and kissed me softly. He tenderly pecked my lips a few times, until I opened my mouth and guided my tongue to meet his. He responded by kissing me harder and holding me closer to him.

We caressed with our tongues and hands, as we inched into the room and allowed the door to close. Neither one of us pulled away. The fever with which we kissed became more and more fierce. He moved his hands from my face to my neck, then over my breasts, squeezing them lightly. I moaned from his touch as my body swayed. David responded with another squeeze and a deeper kiss.

I couldn't remember the last time a kiss evoked such hunger within me. My skin tingled with excitement. I wanted him. But not that way. Not yet. And knowing that I was nearing the point of no return, I pushed away from him and smiled and looked to the ground by his feet.

"Are those for me?"

He smiled, bent down, and picked up the bouquet and gift.

"Well, I was going to give them to this woman I met in the

lobby, but she was allergic to them. So I guess you can have them." He smiled and handed me the roses.

I brought them to my nose and inhaled their fragrance.

On the night of our first date, David had given me two roses. I had kept the petals until my mother threw them away during a cleaning binge.

"They're beautiful," I said softly. I looked at the other gift he held. "Were you going to give that to the woman too?"

"No," he replied with a smirk. "This was for the bellhop, but he had a thing about taking gifts from strangers."

I laughed and walked to a small desk against the far wall. Each rose stem was fitted into a water tube, but I would still have to buy a vase. I laid them down on the desk and turned back to him.

David laid the box on the bed, stepped toward me and took my hands in his. He massaged my fingers just as he used to in the past. His touch was as gentle as ever.

"So," he said softly, "this is it."

"Yes, it is."

We stared in relaxed silence and admired each other's appearance. His boyish looks were still prevalent, though slightly matured. His bedroom eyes were still commanding, and his smile warm and engaging. If there was any one thing about him that had changed, it was his body. Although he had mentioned to me that he went to the gym frequently, I had never imagined that he would be as well-defined and lean as he was. When we saw one another in Philadelphia, I hadn't really taken the time to notice.

I found myself wanting to squeeze his arms and lay my head against his chest, but I held myself back. I smiled at him and exhaled.

"You look beautiful, Jocelyn," David said, running his eyes over my outfit.

I blushed. "Thank you. Why don't we sit down?" I led him to the bed, where we sat side by side with our fingers intertwined. I watched him as he took a moment to peruse the room. He smiled when he saw the candles waiting to be lit.

Candles always took me back to past memories of candlelit dinners and bubble baths. I remembered well the many nights that we spent in the illuminated glow with nothing but love songs to keep us company. We used to talk for hours on end with the music low and peach candles ablaze. I wondered if we would be able to do that again.

"I like the ambiance," he said, turning his attention back to me.

I smiled. "Look at the ceiling."

When David looked to the ceiling, he smiled immediately and laughed.

After satisfying myself, I ran over to the Discovery store in the harbor and bought a pack of glow-in-the-dark stars and stuck them to the ceiling, as we had once done in the past. When the nights were gloomy and we couldn't stare at the real ones outside, David would sneak over to my house, and after making sure my mom was asleep, we'd lay in my bed and whisper softly under the glow of the stickers. Those were always treasured moments for us.

"I've missed you, David."

"I've missed you too," he said quietly. "I've thought about you over and over again since we met in Philly. Ever since we started sending e-mails, I've been dreaming about this moment."

"And how does reality compare to the dream?"

"The dreams were off the hook, but they can't beat the here and now. I've never forgotten about you, Jocelyn. Years may have passed, but you were never out of my mind."

"What made you send me that first e-mail?"

"I gave in."

" 'Gave in'?"

"In the beginning when we first broke up, I couldn't get you off of my mind. I would think about you night and day,

day and night. Every song I heard made me think about you. Everywhere I went would take me back to the times when I'd been out with you. I wrote you endless amounts of letters, telling you how much I loved you and how unhappy I was without you. But I never mailed them."

"Why?"

"Every time I'd get ready to, I'd think about what I did and how much I hurt you, and how you stopped trusting me. Knowing what I put you through kept those letters from being dropped in the mailbox. I just didn't want to bring up ill feelings for you. Eventually as time passed, I moved on and threw them away. But then I saw you in Philly and the strong feelings I had for you came right up. It took me a while to say what I said in that e-mail and send it."

"But eventually you did," I said.

"Like I said, I gave in."

"I'm glad you did." I nestled closer to him and laid my head on his shoulder. "You did hurt me, David. Badly. I hated you for the longest time. Even when I tried to go on without you I hated you. But as much as I hated you, I never stopped loving you. I can't tell you how many times I forced myself to not call you. Saying good-bye was one of the hardest things I'd ever had to do. As time passed, just like you, I moved on."

"And got married," David said in a disappointed tone.

"And you got engaged," I countered.

An uneasy silence fell between us. I was sure neither one of us wanted to mention our partners, yet it was unavoidable and probably best to get it over with. Even though I was happy to be there beside David, guilt was still sitting lightly upon my shoulders. I tried to force it from my mind, but during my wait for David, I had wondered for a brief moment about what Eric was doing. I didn't enjoy hurting him the way I did, but had there really been any other way? I wondered too about what David was feeling inside. Did he regret the lies he had to tell?

"Do you regret this?" I asked, lifting my head. "Do you think this is wrong?"

He looked into my eyes. "I don't know. At this particular moment, I really don't know. It just feels so right being with you."

"But it must feel right being with Janelle too, or else you wouldn't have proposed."

He didn't reply.

"Tell me about her. Is . . ." I paused and thought about what I was about to ask. Finally, in a lower tone, I said, "Is she beautiful?"

David let out a hard breath. "Why do you want to know? I didn't come here to talk about her."

"I'm curious," I answered honestly.

"Why?" He rose from the bed and went to the window.

I watched his reflection in the glass as he stared down at the harbor below.

"Why is knowing anything about her important to you?"

There was so much frustration in his voice that for a second I thought about letting my questions go. But I just couldn't.

"Because before our break-up, I wanted to be the woman who would wear your wedding ring. I'm just curious about the woman who you feel is the one for you. It's almost like she's taken my place."

"She didn't take your place, Jocelyn. No one could have done that."

"Tell me. Please."

He sighed and leaned his forehead against the glass. I hadn't thought of the rendezvous going this way, but I just had to know.

"Yes, she's beautiful," he conceded softly.

I lowered my head. I expected that response, but hearing it was still hard. "Could you spend the rest of your life with her?" I asked with my eyes closed.

"I could spend it with you."

I opened my eyes and looked up at him. "Imagine there's no me," I said, not wanting him to do that at all.

"Kind of hard to do."

"David," I whispered.

"I don't know," he said exhaling. "I just don't know. You're asking me a question that's just too hard for me to answer. Why do you want to know that? What can be gained by that answer? Aren't you happy that you're here? That we're here together?"

I stood up, approached him, and wrapped my arms around his waist. I kissed him on the back of his neck. "I'm sorry to bring this up now. Of course I'm happy being here. I didn't mean or want for you to feel otherwise. To be honest with you, I guess I'm a little jealous. We were together for so long and shared so much."

"And we're together right now," he said, turning around. "This was a big decision for both of us to make, but now that we've made it, I don't want to waste the time away. We have a lot of catching up to do, I know. There are a lot of questions that are going to have to be answered. A lot of important, life-changing decisions that are going to have to be made. But I don't want to do that right now. Right now, all I want is to feel you in my arms and know that my dream is now a reality. I screwed up before. I will always remember that."

"We were kids. That's all in the past. Damn it, I love you so much. I may not have wanted to admit it, but I knew it when we parted in Philadelphia. I knew it when I read the e-mail. And I knew it the moment I opened that door."

He leaned forward and kissed me. "Open your gift," he said. He took me by the hand and led me back to the bed, where he picked up the box and handed it to me. "I hope you still like these."

I took the present and unwrapped it in breathless anticipation. He watched me and smiled as I removed a porcelain mask from the box.

"Oh . . ."

It was painted in a glossy white. The eyes and the nose were hidden behind a visor of feathers. The lips were painted in red and lined in gold. It wore a rapturous smile.

"This is beautiful. I haven't gotten one of these in years." I hugged and kissed him and admired it a few more times, then carefully placed it in the box and laid it on the floor.

David took me in his arms. "I love you, Jocelyn. Always have, always will."

Our kiss this time was greedy and uninhibited. I moaned as he slid his hand through my slit and caressed my naked thigh. He slowly worked his way up and in between my thighs, our tongues dancing to a slow rhythm. I parted my legs to allow room for him to fondle and laid my hand over his crotch, feeling him harden and grow. I giggled like a schoolgirl as he throbbed beneath his clothing.

Without removing my hand, I gently forced him to lie back on the bed. I could tell that he was close to the point of explosion. With a seductive smile, I rose and stepped away from the bed, giving him a full view of me.

I swayed my hips in slow, sensuous circles, and ran my hands down the sides of my thighs. I performed for him and removed my dress, letting him admire the contours of my body. His eyes were focused on me as I removed my strapless bra and matching thong.

When I was completely naked, David stood and removed his clothing. I felt like a teenager about to lose my virginity. I couldn't remember the last time I felt as excited. I gasped when his boxers slid to the floor, allowing his member to stand at full attention.

With seduction in my stride, I approached and mounted him, but didn't allow him to slide inside of me. I wanted to make him wait. I wanted myself to wait. I stared down at him and passed my hands over his chest. The hairs on my arms rose; the gym had served him well.

He sat up and gently caressed my breasts and squeezed my nipples, which were erect with excitement. At that moment, gone from my mind were any feelings of guilt or doubt I may have had. My heart was beating from the sheer masculine scent of him.

He took hold of the hair behind my neck and pulled me down. I breathed out when he ran his tongue from my nipple to the underside of my chin. I licked his neck and savored the taste of his skin. I kissed him lightly and sucked on his bottom lip. He returned with a nibble of his own.

The air between us was electric and rising in temperature with each caress. I passed my hands down along his back, admiring the feel and tautness of his muscles. I couldn't resist him any longer. I slowly guided him inside of me, his thickness causing me to inhale deeply. I felt his breath blow hot against me as he embraced me around my waist and brought my body flush against his. We moved together to a tune that only we could hear, and for the next few hours, we put the song on repeat.

David slept quietly as I lay at ease in his arms. Despite the years apart, our lovemaking hadn't changed. We still knew each other's body like no one else did. Only he could make me scream during an orgasm, and that night had been no exception. I couldn't remember the last time I came like that. I nestled myself deeper into his arms. He stirred for a moment and then fell still again.

In the silence, I thought of my current life with Eric. Despite everything I felt for him, I had always known there was something missing, some critical piece that kept me one step away from contentment. There, lying in David's arms, I found what I'd been searching for.

Marc

I was showering, when my cell phone went off. Without turning the water off, I stepped out of the shower and rushed to answer the phone. Water dripped from my body to the hardwood flooring. I was expecting a call from Dahlia. I had to postpone the trip to my parents for a day because she had to work the night before. I hadn't been able to get her off my mind. Taking her to meet my parents was going to be a first for me. I'd never taken any of the women I'd dated to meet my parents because I had never been serious about any of them. The thought of the relationship moving beyond anything sexual never crossed my mind. I never saw the possibility of a future with any of them.

But Dahlia was different. Not only could I imagine myself growing old with her, I could also picture us raising a family together. I wanted my parents to see that. Especially my mother, who, for years, had been harassing me about settling down with the right woman and giving her a grandchild. My father didn't care one way or the other. Before he met my mother, he too had been a playboy of sorts, so he understood my restlessness.

"Dahlia, Dahlia," I hummed.

At first, I didn't know what to do when I saw Dave's home phone number on my caller ID. Dave was in Maryland by this time, but, technically, we were supposed to have been at my parents' place. I thought of letting my voice mail take the call but decided against it. Janelle knew that I always answered my cell, and I didn't want to give her any reason for suspicion, especially since Dave didn't have his phone. I pressed the talk button and prayed that somehow it would be David calling to tell me that he had decided to do the right thing and had cancelled the trip.

"Talk to me."

"Hey, Marc," Janelle said.

No such luck. "Hey, Janelle. What's going on?"

"Not much. I'm busy trying to catch up on my work."

"Right, right. Work. It just won't go away."

Janelle laughed. "No, it won't at all."

We both laughed and then there was a few seconds of silence. I wanted nothing more than to get off the phone.

Finally, Janelle spoke. "So how are your parents doing?"

I shook my head. When I first met Janelle, I found her to be self-absorbed and uptight. I didn't like her West Coast attitude. It was almost as if she thought she was better than everyone else. On the other side of the coin, she thought I was a womanizer and insensitive, which was right. But what bothered me was how she was always questioning Dave about the merits of our friendship. She was actually worried that my ways were going to pass on to him.

At one point, to avoid an argument, Dave made sure that Janelle and I were never at the same place. But as their relationship grew stronger, I realized she wasn't going to go away, and although I had to bite my tongue a lot of times, I found a way to be cool with her.

Eventually we became friends, and I found that once she let her initial guard down, she was a far more considerate and sociable person than she showed. Her heart was as big as his was, and she gave me a woman's point of view on different subjects. I never told Dave, but it was Janelle who gave me advice on how to pursue Dahlia.

Now, I was faced with having to lie to her, which I would do, because Dave was my boy and I wouldn't betray that friendship.

"It's not pretty over here, but at least no one's dead yet."

"Yeah, I guess that is a good thing. Is your mother okay?"

"She's pissed as hell and she's hurting, but she's hanging in there." I stared at the water puddling around my feet. I felt myself drowning with each lie. "She's a strong woman."

"She has to be. She dealt with you," Janelle quipped.

"Yeah, no doubt about that."

"Anyway, can I speak to David for a minute?"

I hesitated for a second and hoped that she didn't notice. Dave warned me that she might call since he left his cell, so I was prepared, but ashamed. "You just missed him. He just left and took my parents to get something to eat. I was taking a shower when you called."

"Oh," Janelle said. "I was hoping to speak with him. Well, can you tell him I called, and when he gets a chance, for him to call me?"

"Sure thing."

"Thanks."

"No problem. I'll talk to you later."

As I prepared to end the call, I heard Janelle call my name.

I cursed under my breath. "What's up?"

"I just wanted to ask you something."

"Go ahead."

"Is Dahlia what you expected?"

I smiled as the hairs on my skin stood straight. "She's more," I said proudly.

"Good. You know, Marc, I may not have thought so in the

beginning, but I can't imagine David having a better friend than you, and never in a million years would I have guessed the type of friend you would've become to me. I'm glad we got to know each other."

"So am I." I bit down on my bottom lip after saying that. The happiness in her voice was beating the shit out of my conscience.

"Remember to tell David to call me. I'll talk to you later."

Janelle hung up the phone, leaving me wet and disheartened. "I hope you know what you're doing, bruh." I sighed, dropped the phone on the couch, and walked back to the bathroom.

David

When I got home, I closed my car door, leaned against it, and looked up at the night sky. I sighed. The weekend spent with Jocelyn had been perfect. During our time together we took strolls along the harbor and dined at different restaurants. When we weren't out, we were in the suite, talking or making love. And when we weren't talking or filling the room with passion, we lay in each other's arms and didn't say a word. I hadn't intended on leaving so late for my drive back to New York, but it had been nearly impossible to leave her side. When we said good-bye, plans had been made for another meeting.

I looked away from the sky and checked my watch. It showed three a.m. I knew that the hard part had now arrived. I had never cheated on Janelle before. I didn't want to face her just yet, so if she was asleep, which she should have been, I would just camp out on the couch in front of the television. I grabbed my bag, and as I walked, I went over the lies I had formulated during the drive home.

I slept on the couch with the television on as I had planned on doing, but in the morning I still didn't want to deal with her, so I left before she woke up.

I went to the gym and had a mediocre workout then went to see my agent, Diane. She harassed me about my new book, which I hadn't written half of yet, and reminded me that the deadline was coming soon. I hated the pressure of having to write. I liked to let the thoughts come naturally. But still, I had to admit, I had been bullshitting about it. And now with Jocelyn in the picture, writing was the last thing I had on my mind.

When I finally worked up the nerve and after having walked around Manhattan for a while, I hopped on the subway and went home.

As I walked through the door, Janelle was just sitting down at the table to eat dinner by herself. It was the first time that we had seen each other. I gave her a kiss on the forehead as I joined her at the table.

She never responded.

During our meal, we sat across from one another and ate in almost complete silence. If it wasn't for the silverware grazing across the flatware, I think we could've heard a pin drop.

"I got your note this morning," Janelle said. There was a hint of anger in her voice. "Why didn't you wake me up when you came home?"

"I wasn't tired last night, and I knew if I woke you up, you wouldn't have been able to go back to sleep."

"And what about this morning?"

"I had some things to take care of."

"Before seven?"

"I went to the gym then had a meeting with Diane. I may have to do some more traveling in the coming weeks."

"You could've said hello. You may not have missed me, but I missed you."

"I'm sorry," I said, taking her hand in mine. "I was trying to be considerate. And I did miss you. It was just a hectic weekend." I caressed her fingers, which she normally loved.

She pulled her hand away and grabbed her glass. Taking a long sip, she looked at me with fire in her eyes. And it wasn't the kind of fire that I liked. "You forgot your cell phone."

"Yeah, I realized once I was halfway down the turnpike."

"I called Marc's phone. Didn't he tell you?"

I called Marc once from the hotel, and he told me that she had called, so I knew this was coming. I set my fork down and exhaled. "No, he didn't tell me. He must have forgotten. Like I said, it was hectic. Dealing with his parents wasn't easy."

"So you never even thought to call and make sure your fiancée was okay?" she asked with an edge.

I had to get away from the table. I couldn't bear to look at her. "Look, did you think the weekend was going to be a walk in the park for Marc and me? I'm sorry that I didn't call you, all right? And I'm sorry that I didn't wake you up. I came home late, and you're just not the friendliest person when you're tired. Now, can we please eat and talk about something else?"

She slammed her palm on the dining table, causing my glass to nearly topple over. "Talk about something else? What do you want to talk about?"

"Anything but this."

"Oh, really? Okay, well since things always have to go the way *you* want it, why don't you tell me what we're going to talk about? Work? How about that? Or maybe we should talk about sports. You like sports, don't you?"

"Janelle . . ."

"What? You don't like those topics? Well, here's one for you. Maybe we should talk about the fact that yesterday marked our fourth anniversary since we started dating. I mean, I know we're not married, but I thought that *was* something important. You're quiet now. Is this not a good topic for you?"

Oh shit. Our anniversary.

Before I could respond, she pushed herself away from the table and removed a small box hidden beneath a napkin.

"Here's your fucking present," she said, throwing the box at me. "Happy fucking anniversary."

Without another word she stormed off, leaving me there alone with my shame. I felt terrible. I had completely forgotten that our anniversary was that weekend.

I locked my fingers together on top of my head and leaned back in my chair. I could hear her cursing from the bedroom. I looked at the box. It was small and square. I reluctantly picked it up and removed the wrapping around it. When I opened it, I felt damn small. Inside was an onyx ring that I'd had my eye on. I was going to buy it one day, but before I could, Janelle rushed me out of the store for something. Now I knew why.

I removed the ring and enclosed it in my palm. My dream had just ended. I was now having my nightmare.

After the disaster with Janelle, I had to get out, and Marc's was the one place I knew I could go to and be free to wallow in my guilt.

"You look like shit, bruh. Was the weekend that good?"

I walked into Marc's condo and, without saying a word, headed straight for the alcohol. I poured a shot of vodka and downed it without hesitation.

He looked at me. He knew something was wrong. (I never drank hard liquor.)

"All right, bruh, what happened? Did Janelle find out? What'd you do, forget to cover up a hickey?"

I took another shot then walked to his couch and slumped into it. "Worse. Yesterday was our anniversary. I forgot."

"Oh shit." Marc went to his bar and downed a shot of his own. He came back and plopped down beside me with the bottle in his hand.

I looked at him and then held out my hand to show him the ring. "She bought me this."

Marc looked at the ring and shook his head. "Damn."

"Yeah."

We sat in silence and, between the two of us, finished the rest of the bottle. I don't remember when I fell asleep.

Janelle

"I'm sorry, girl."

I held the phone to my ear and tissue to my eyes. I couldn't stop crying. I couldn't believe that David actually forgot.

"I expected him to come home and make it up to me, girl. I never would've believed that he would forget." I wiped the tears from my eyes and took a deep angry breath.

After he left, I walked around the house, cursing. And when he didn't come home, I cried until my head hurt. Finally, when I had nothing but dry tears left, I called my girl Tina in California to tell her what happened.

She'd met David when we flew out to Cali for a mini-vacation. She liked him instantly, which I knew she would. I even think she flirted with him a couple of times, but that was ok because Tina couldn't help herself. When a good-looking man was around, Tina Jordan-Dickinson's Caribbean wiles suddenly seemed to emerge. Her parents were Jamaican, but she was born and raised in California. Her skin was the color of dark chocolate and as smooth as satin. She had the kind of figure men loved—large breasts, wide hips, and a rear end to sit on. Men could never resist her, but I knew I had nothing to worry about with David.

"He didn't even apologize, girl. Can you believe that shit?"

Tina sucked her teeth. "Just like a man."

Angry tears fell from my eyes. They wouldn't stop coming.

"What are you going to do?" she asked.

"I don't know. He left last night without a word. He's probably at Marc's place right now."

"Are you sure about that?"

"Of course, I'm sure. Why are you asking me that?"

"Look, girl, I know you love your man, and I know he's a good man, but he's a man nonetheless."

"What are you implying?"

"Janelle, I'm not saying anything is going on or that he would do anything behind your back, but just keep your guard up, okay? I know more than anyone does how easy men can fall for a batting eyelash and a wiggling of the booty. Just don't be so naïve that you make yourself blind."

" 'Naïve'? Tina, I know how men are. I know what they're capable of. But I know that I don't have to worry about that with David."

"Janelle—" Tina started.

I cut her off. "Tina, I thought about the possibility of that happening, but I let it go because I know that David loves me and he would never do anything to hurt me."

"All right, Janelle. I'm just being your best friend, girl. That's exactly why I'm telling you this. I don't want to see you get hurt. Just keep your eyes open. That's all I'm saying."

I remained silent for a long while. There was a lot of truth to what she had said, but I didn't want to believe that David was like all the rest of the men out there. He wouldn't betray me like that. He had more respect for me than that. Didn't he?

"Tina, I've got to go."

"Girl, I know you're not too thrilled about what I'm saying, and that's okay. I'm glad you have that much faith in your man, but I'm just saying that it can happen. Hell, Derrick did it to me last year."

"What?"

"Yeah, with some skank-ass bitch from the office. She wanted money. The bitch called here one day and threatened him over the phone. Said she would tell me everything if he didn't pay up. He didn't know I was listening on the other end."

"What happened?"

"He paid her—that's what happened. Two hundred thousand fucking dollars. He said he lost it in some deal. But it's a drop in the bucket for him—for us. Shit, I'm not exactly going to win any awards for purity myself, you know. I figured I could live with it. I'm not trying to lose what I have, you know? I just watch his ass like a hawk now. He can't do shit without me knowing. To be honest, I think he knows, because he gives me whatever the hell I ask for. 'You want money, honey? You want my credit cards? Do you want my dick now?' Ha!"

"You're crazy."

"Crazy I am."

"I'm sorry that happened," I said quietly. I couldn't believe that Derrick had done that. If he could, could David? No. I couldn't believe that.

"It's no biggie," Tina said, feigning indifference.

But I could hear an edge in her voice that I hadn't heard before. She wasn't as over it as she pretended.

"I'm just telling you to be on your guard. I'm not trying to destroy the perception you have of David. I'm sure he's as good as you say he is. Just remember, nothing is impossible."

After hanging up the phone, I sat alone in the living room and stared at photographs of David and me. I looked at his smile and stared at his lips. I didn't know what I would do if he ever betrayed me and put his lips on someone else. I felt sorry for Tina, but I couldn't help thinking about how the things we did always seemed to come back around to bite us twofold. I guess it was just her turn.

I tried to call David on his cell phone, but I got his voice mail. I didn't leave a message. I thought of calling Marc's condo, but I knew that I would only have been doing that because of what Tina told me. I didn't want to start mistrusting him, so I decided to wait until he got home.

Jocelyn

I looked at the clock and wondered how things went for David. I had the hotel room for one additional day. I just wanted some time to myself to think. I lay back on the bed and stared up at the ceiling.

The weekend had been something out of a dream; a dream that I had imagined happening just as it did. Only, in my fantasy, David never left.

Teardrops fell from the corners of my eyes. Even with the lapse of time, things between us hadn't changed. Our connection was as strong as ever. If anything, it had gotten stronger, more intense.

Just as he did in the past, David had managed to steal my heart again.

But still, part of me felt guilty for enjoying it as much as I did. In the back of my mind, I remembered that I was still married. I had made that commitment. But for how long could I go on without David?

The flow of tears increased and dampened the pillow beneath my head. I couldn't go back home. Was my marriage over?

Webs and Lies

Jocelyn

Three Months Later

"Eric came by the house again," Marisol said, finishing her dinner.

I put my glass down and shook my head.

After my weekend with David, I had tried to go home to Eric, but it was impossible to remain civil. We began to argue almost immediately.

"Jocelyn, why are you so against the idea of raising a family?"

"Please, Eric, let's not start this again. Obviously our problems are much bigger to me than they are to you."

"Damn it! Did you think we wouldn't have problems? We *can* fix things. We said 'through good and bad times,' remember?"

"I need time to think, Eric. I need some space. I'm moving in with Marisol for a little while."

"But Jocelyn—"

"I think it would be best for both of us right now."

Since I left he had been calling and coming by periodically, trying to convince me to move back home.

"I can't say I blame him," Mari continued. "You need to do something."

I exhaled. *"¿Qué quieres que haga, Mari?"*

"Tell him the truth."

"I can't do that."

"So you'd rather hurt him?"

"Look, I'm not trying to hurt him. I just know that it would do more harm to him if I told him the truth."

"Okay, so until you do that, you'd rather have him coming by on hands and knees, begging you to come home? That's nice of you. I'm sure he would appreciate that."

"Damn it, why are you giving me such a hard time? I'm happy. You should be concerning yourself with that. I'm *your* sister."

"Sí, and he's my brother-in-law, who I care for. Shit, if it doesn't work out for you two, that's fine. But don't string him along. That's all I'm trying to say."

"I'm not trying to string him along."

"But you are, Jocelyn. Every time he calls and you refuse to take his calls, every time he comes by and you won't see him, you do that. You know that your heart is somewhere else. You know that you love someone else. Just let Eric go, and then you'll have nothing to worry about. Or will you?"

"What does that mean?"

She rose from the table and took her plate to the sink.

"What do you mean by that?" I persisted.

She put her plate down and turned toward me. "Have you thought about what David is going to do? I don't see him changing his life the way you have. He still has a home with a fiancée, who he is *still* making wedding plans with. Is he planning on ending his relationship?"

"It's not that easy."

" 'Not that easy'? You're the one who's married! He can up and leave whenever he wants to."

"I don't want to talk about this."

"That's your problem. *You* want. *You* don't want. It's all about *you*. You want to have your cake and eat it too. I love you, sis, but you're being selfish."

I slammed my hand on the table and stood up. I couldn't believe that she was going off on me like this. "Damn it, what the hell is up with you? I haven't been happy like this in a long time. Why are you jumping all over me like this?"

"Let me ask you something, Jocelyn—how the hell can you be so in love with David?"

"What kind of question is that?"

"I mean, how can you be so head over heels with him? Do you want me to say it in Spanish? You guys dated for a while, then you broke up for over six years. How can you have fallen in love with him so quickly? I don't understand."

I looked away from her and stared at my reflection in a glass fruit bowl on the table. My face was wide and distorted and looked nothing like me. I wondered if David would love me in the same way if I looked differently. Something inside me told me that he would.

"You may not understand this, but he's my soul mate. He completes me in a way that no one else has, or could."

"Didn't Eric do that too? You married him."

I glared at my sister. She was really beginning to piss me off. I grabbed my purse. I didn't want to continue with the conversation. "David and I were meant to be together. That's all there is to it."

"Too bad you didn't tell Eric before you married him."

"Go to hell, Mari," I said, walking out of the kitchen.

I got my own apartment a week later.

Janelle

David left for another business weekend again. He'd been doing that a lot lately. Always leaving to meet with different people and see different areas for research. We'd barely spoken to each other, and our intimacy was nowhere close to being what it used to be. He'd even been sleeping on the couch some nights, right in front of his laptop.

Being an editor, I knew how the writing process worked. I knew that when a writer got the urge, he had to jump on it. But I was really beginning to hate that damn PC. He'd been spending more time with it than me. I knew he was having problems with his new book, which he still hadn't told me about.

I was starting to get really worried. Even all the discussions about our wedding had ceased. Shit, my own parents talked about it more than David and I did. Of course, they had no clue about the problems he and I were having.

I'd talked with Tina several times, and each time I did, she never hesitated to make me question his character. Of course, I defended my man, but in the back of my mind I couldn't help wondering.

Stress was definitely getting the better of me. I couldn't do my job properly. I'd broken out in hives once, and to make matters worse, I was pregnant. I didn't want to admit it at first. I kept telling myself that the nausea and sudden cravings for ice cream were due to the anxiety, but I could only lie to myself for so long.

Pregnant. Three months at that.

David and I had become so distant that he didn't even notice my morning sickness. *I wonder what he would think about the news?* Would he embrace the idea of being a father? What would this do to our relationship? I wasn't even sure what direction it was heading. We seemed to be spiraling toward rock bottom. Maybe the baby would help. Maybe it wouldn't. The fact that the answers weren't right there for me to see only frustrated me more. I knew one thing though: no matter how David felt, no matter what his reaction was, I was about to become a mommy. I held off on telling him; I just wasn't ready. But I needed to tell someone.

"You're what?" Tina asked, her voice full of shock.

"Pregnant," I mumbled.

"Damn, girl, that's what I thought you said. Well, congratulations! And what was Prince Charming's reaction?"

I hesitated before I answered her. And when I did, I hurried through my response. "He doesn't know." I didn't have to be there to know Tina was scowling on the other end.

"Oh, Lord. You didn't tell him?"

"I can't right now. I don't know how to. Things have been so bad."

"Girl, you have to tell him."

"I know," I said with a sigh. I don't know if it was because my hormones were out of whack, but I was really scared of losing David. "Tina, I just don't know what he would say or do."

"Shit, he better do what all those other brothers out there

won't do. He better say, 'Whoopee,' and start buying Pampers and milk."

We laughed, but then things got serious again.

"Listen, Janelle, you're my girl. I'm there for you no matter what. But I'm telling you, if you don't tell that brother now, things will get worse. Shit, it's bad enough he's having an affair."

"Tina! For the umpteenth time, he's not having an affair. Please don't start that shit again."

"Janelle, Janelle, Janelle. Will you just listen to yourself? You're in denial, girl. He's showing all the classic signs of a man on a mission. He goes away on weekends. Why? Because of work. He stays up all night on his laptop. Why? To write his book. I bet his ass is writing. Writing her, maybe."

"Tina, please." This was the last topic I wanted to discuss.

"Girl, when was the last time you and David fucked? Can you tell me that?"

I remained silent for a long while. Her last question bit me right to the core. As much as I denied that David was being unfaithful, I had asked myself that last question too. But I didn't want to admit that to Tina.

"Tina, I'm pregnant. The last thing I feel like doing is having sex."

"Okay, I'll give you that one, but tell me this then—when was the last time David tried to fuck you?"

I didn't answer right away.

At one point David used to always try to get me in bed. But with Tina's question, I realized for the first time that I couldn't remember the last time David made moves on me.

My silence was all the answer Tina needed. "Mmm hmmm. There you go," she said in her I-told-you-so tone. "Girl, I love you, so I'll always tell you the truth, even if it hurts. But if your man ain't fucking you, he's fucking someone else."

"Tina, please. He's not sleeping with some other bitch."

"You keep telling yourself that, Janelle."

"I will, because it's true," I demanded with absolutely no conviction.

"Girl, the truth ain't easy to swallow. You need to find out what your man is up to before you get hurt. Listen to what I'm saying, Janelle."

As much as I didn't want to, I was really starting to digest her logic. Why hadn't David tried to have sex with me? Why did he have to go away so frequently? What if she was right?

I sat and sulked for a long while after I hung up the phone. Then I looked at David's laptop sitting alone in the corner. I knew his password to access his e-mail. What if he wasn't writing his book?

I inched my way toward the laptop but stopped just as my fingers rested on the cover. What if he was writing his book? What if he wasn't being unfaithful? Our relationship was built on trust and whether he knew it or not, I didn't want to destroy that. I shook my head and moved my fingers away. Damn Tina and damn David. I left the laptop alone and went to take a shower. I had a lot of thinking to do.

Eric

"Is our marriage over?"

I didn't want to ask that question, but I had no choice. Since the blowup, Jocelyn had moved in with her sister, avoided my calls and eventually gotten her own apartment. Getting her own place really shocked the hell out of me. That was the last thing I expected to find out. I was just glad her sister told me.

I'd always had a good relationship with Mari. We were both alike in a lot of ways. I just wished that she wasn't caught in the middle of the problems Jocelyn and I were having. It wasn't fair to her, but I blame Jocelyn for that.

As hard as it was, I could bring myself to understand why she didn't want a baby. Maybe we weren't ready. Maybe we did have a lot of issues to clear up before moving on to that level of responsibility. But even if that was the case, why did she take things to the extreme? What made her go off and leave me like that? Could there be someone else?

No longer satisfied with Jocelyn not wanting to provide answers, I went to Mari's house to get some information. For the first time in months, she actually let me in. And when we sat down at her kitchen table, I could tell by the look on her face that I wasn't going to like what I heard.

"Jocelyn doesn't stay here anymore," she said before I could ask her anything.

"What? Where is she?"

"She got her own apartment."

I didn't say a word for a couple of seconds. Finally, I said, "What's going on, Mari?"

Mari sighed and looked back at me with frustration in her eyes. "I don't know. Jocelyn won't open up to me."

I lowered my head and sighed. "I thought things were okay, you know? I mean, we had problems, but what couples don't?"

"Well, I guess the problems were bigger than you thought. I don't know what to tell you, Eric. I've talked to her. I've tried to get her to talk to you. But she can be a stubborn ass sometimes. You know that."

I didn't want to ask my next question, but I had no choice. "Is she seeing someone else? I know she's your sister and you're loyal to her, but I need to know."

Mari stared at me before she replied. I could see in her eyes that she was holding out on me, and I knew that whatever it was, she wasn't going to tell me. Like they say, blood is thicker than water.

"No."

"Mari . . . please," I tried.

"No, Eric, she's not."

"Then what the hell is it? What made her do all of this? I can't believe that our problems were that bad."

"Look, I don't know what to tell you. I guess Jocelyn just wasn't as happy as you thought she was. I really don't want to get any more involved than I already am. This is between you two."

"I understand. Believe me, Mari, I don't like the fact that you're involved any more than you do. But you are involved, like it or not."

"I don't."

"Where is she staying?"

"I can't tell you. You know that."

"Come on, Mari. She's my wife."

"I'm sorry, Eric, but I can't tell you."

"At least give me her number."

"I can't."

"You're the only point of contact I have. If I can't get to her directly, then I have to come through you. I know you don't want that. All I'm asking for is the number. Is it listed?"

"No."

"Okay. Then I can't get her address from it. Just give it to me, please. At least give me the ability to talk to her. I *need* to talk to her."

I held my breath and clenched my teeth. I knew that getting the number was a long shot. As close as they were, the last thing Mari would've ever done was betray her sister.

I stared at her hard, refusing to let her gaze fall away from mine, and then I took her hand in mine. "Please," I begged.

When Mari exhaled, I knew she had given in.

"You know she's going to hate me for this."

"But I love you," I said, trying to lighten the mood.

"Yeah, well, that won't help any."

I left her house with Jocelyn's number in my pocket. When I got home, I thought about what I would say. But I had no idea. I thought about my question to Mari. Was Jocelyn seeing anyone? My gut told me yes, but I tried to ignore it. I couldn't believe that. I didn't want to believe that our bond could be broken. So I called. And when I got her answering machine, I asked the first question that came to my mind. *Is our marriage over?* Unfortunately, I didn't like the answer that I gave myself.

Marisol

"Why the hell did you give Eric my number?"

Oh, Lord. I knew that was coming. But what else could I do? He was my brother-in-law, and although she was my blood, I still didn't think what she was doing was right. I never thought that things with David would have gone as far as they did. I figured their weekend together was going to be nothing more than that—just a weekend. A fling. Wham, bam, thank you, ma'am, and have a nice life. See you in another six years.

I almost stumbled when Eric asked me if she was having an affair. He looked so sad and worn, with heavy circles under his eyes. It even looked like he had lost some weight.

Damn. I hate to see people go through crap like that. I remember how hard it was for me when I had to deal with the physical abuse from my ex-husband. I knew all about the heavy circles and weight loss. Even though their situation might not have been as grave as mine was, it was still awful—in some ways worse. At least with the abuse, I knew where things stood. He was a bastard, and that's all there was to it. I didn't cause any of it to happen. But with Eric, he had no idea what

Jocelyn was doing. He had his suspicions though. His imagination. And that alone was enough.

"You need to come clean, Jocelyn."

"How do you know what I need? Damn it, Mari. How could you?"

"How could I? You mean, how could *you?* Do you have any idea what you're putting him through? He looks terrible, Jocelyn. Why are you doing this to him? So he works a lot. So fucking what! He loves you. He's a good man." I stopped talking because I could feel myself on the verge of going off on her, something I hadn't done in a long time.

Damn, I should have never helped her.

"It's more than him working long hours, and you know that."

"Okay, so there are problems. Fix them and move on. You're selling yourself short if you think you'll find complete happiness with David."

"How do you know that I haven't already?"

"Please," I said curtly. "Don't waste your breath on me. Happiness, my ass. All you've found is a weekend bedroom buddy."

"Shut up!" she screamed.

I could hear her choking up over the phone, and I was glad that I couldn't see her, because I couldn't stop. She had to hear the truth, and it was better for it to come from someone who cared.

"No, you shut up and listen! If you're so happy, then tell Eric you want a divorce. Then you can do whatever you want, wherever you want with David. Of course, there's that little problem called David's fiancée. But I'm sure he'll end that relationship too."

Jocelyn was crying on the other end now, and I hated every minute of it, but I had to press on.

"David is planning on doing that, right? I mean, seeing as how he loves you so much."

I stopped speaking then and listened to my sister cry. I felt like the big bully beating up on the scrawny kid in the school playground.

"Look," I said with a softer tone, "I love you. I don't want to see you get hurt, but I think you are setting yourself up for failure with David. You two may love each other, but it can't work. At least not the way it's going now. I just don't want you to give up someone as good as Eric. At least talk to him. You owe him that much."

She didn't say a word to me and hung up the phone.

I hoped that I had gotten through to her in some way. I was happy that she was happy, but at the same time, I really didn't see a future for her and David—not as long as he still had his relationship. My only hope was that Jocelyn would realize that before it was too late.

David

Jocelyn,

This won't be long. I just wanted to tell you that I miss you like crazy. I can't tell you enough how happy I have been these last couple of months. I can't wait for the time when we can spend more than just weekends together. I'm glad we took the chance. I hope you are too. I know you want more time from me, and I promise that will come very soon. I promise. I'll write more later.

Love Always,
David

I sent the e-mail and then clicked over to my Word document. I finally managed to finish another unfulfilling chapter in my new thriller about a serial killer determined to ruin the career of an esteemed New York detective. I had finished seven chapters in all but was on the verge of throwing it all away. My agent was going to kill me. I knew that I was going to miss my deadline, and I had never done that before. I just didn't have a good feeling for the story like I have had in the past. Truthfully, I was too happy to care.

Jocelyn and I had taken every opportunity possible to see each other. Actually, now that she had her own apartment, the task had really fallen on me to get away, but I always managed. Every now and then, I thought about her marriage and wondered if I had been the cause of their break up.

Jocelyn always insisted I wasn't. She said that the end had been a long time coming. That she was never truly happy until we found one another again.

I was busy staring at my book on the computer screen when Janelle came home.

She looked at me and gave me a half-smile.

Ever since I forgot our anniversary, eggshells had been laying all over the apartment. Although I'd tried to make it up to her, I knew that she hadn't let it go. To tell the truth, I hadn't either. I still cared for her, and hurting her was not something I wanted to do.

"David." She walked toward me with purpose in her eyes. "We need to talk."

I looked up from my laptop. I really didn't feel like talking because, somehow, we always wound up going at each other's throats.

"Can this wait? I'm in the middle of something right now."

She stood with her hand on her hips and her lips curled. I couldn't tell if she was mad, sad, or glad. Then she hit me with a blow from down under. "I'm pregnant."

Time seemed to freeze after she said that, because nothing moved—not even me. I sat silent and listened to the sounds of my heartbeat and my own breathing, which had both been amplified.

I must have said something, because Janelle nodded and said, "Yes, I'm sure. Four months pregnant."

Four months! Four months? "How?" I thought, but managed to say out loud.

"What do you mean, 'How?' What kind of question is that?"

"When?"

"Four months ago, obviously."

"And you're sure?"

"I went to the doctor."

I sat still, unable to say much else. *Pregnant.* The word just kept repeating itself over and over in my head. *Pregnant, pregnant, pregnant.* Oh shit. "Whose is it?"

"What?" Janelle yelled out. "I know you didn't just ask me that! What the hell do you mean who? Who do you think? I can't believe you had the nerve to ask me a question like that!"

"Janelle . . ."

"Janelle, nothing. Let's keep it real, David. Maybe I should be asking you the same question. Who have you been sleeping with?"

"What do you mean by that?"

"I meant exactly what I said. Who have you been fucking? Because it sure hasn't been me."

"Come on, don't be ridiculous."

" 'Ridiculous'? I had to start using my goddamned sex toy again just to keep my lonely ass company! Your attention has to be going somewhere or to someone. So which is it? Or better yet, maybe I should ask, 'What's the bitch's name'?"

I stood up and grabbed my jacket from the coat closet. "I don't need this shit." I wanted to get the hell out of there. I needed to think. *Pregnant? Shit.*

"I don't need your bullshit accusations."

"That's right, David. Leave just like a man. Who knows, maybe you can go and see her. Maybe she can make your ass feel better. Just don't forget to tell her that I'm pregnant."

I walked out without saying a word. In the hallway, waiting for the elevator, I could hear only one thing—a baby crying from the condo next door.

Marc

"She's fucking pregnant," Dave said, walking right past me when I opened the door.

Dahlia and I were watching a movie, when he called me from his cell phone. We'd been seeing each other almost every day. She even quit the gym and went to work at another one, because she said it was too uncomfortable, with me being her boss. I agreed.

We alternated evenings at each other's place, and it had been her turn by me that night. I hated for her to leave, but Dave sounded like a wreck on the phone. Now I knew why.

"Say that again, bruh," I said as I closed the door.

He threw his coat on the couch and began to pace back and forth.

"Please tell me that I heard you wrong. Jocelyn is pregnant?"

"Nah, not Jocelyn, Janelle. She's four fucking months pregnant." He started burning trails in my hardwood floor again.

"Damn." I went for the bottle of vodka and handed it to him. "You look like you need this more than I do."

Dave took a long sip.

"Shit, how did you find out?"

"She just told me."

"Damn. What are you going to do?"

He continued to pace and shook his head. "I don't know. Shit, I just don't know."

"Oh, man," I said, falling into my couch, not knowing what I would have done in his position.

"There's something else." He sat down beside me. "She accused me of cheating on her."

"Oh damn," I whispered. "She knows?"

"No, she doesn't know shit. She just accused me of it."

"Women can sense those things, man. It's part of their genetics. That's why we always get caught. So what did you say?"

"I denied it, of course. I told her she was being ridiculous."

"Then what?"

"Then I left. I just grabbed my jacket, and here I am, wallowing in pity next to your ass."

"Shit. What about Jocelyn?"

"What about her?"

"You've got to tell her."

"I don't even want to think about that yet."

"You have to. I mean, Janelle is going to keep it, right?"

"We haven't even gotten that far, but I think she will. She wouldn't abort her baby."

"You ready to be a father?"

"Shit, I have no choice."

"Damn," I whispered.

I felt for him. I really did, but I won't front, he brought this shit on himself. Ever since he and Jocelyn started to get more and more involved, I tried to give him advice. I told him that he had to pick one or the other before the shit hit the fan. Well, the fan was clogged and funky now.

"You're gonna have to tell Jocelyn. And soon."

He got up and started his pacing again. "Marc," he said between sips, "if I tell her, I might lose her."

"You have to do it, bruh. You can't keep this a secret. You know that. And don't tell her in an e-mail either."

David suddenly screamed out, "Oh shit!"

"What the . . . What's wrong now? Damn. You trying to give a brother a heart attack?"

"Oh shit, oh shit, oh shit, oh shit," he recited over and over.

From the tone in his voice, I knew I didn't want to know what it was. "What is it, man? What now?"

He came back to the couch, sat down and laid his elbows on his knees and bowed his head.

I had to strain to hear what he said next.

"Before Janelle came in, I was working on my new novel. When she wanted to speak, I closed the lid down."

"Okay. And?"

"I never turned it off."

I shrugged my shoulders. "Okay."

"Along with my Word document, my Outlook was still open. I left it open in case Jocelyn responded right away. If an e-mail comes, Janelle's going to hear the chime. She's already suspicious. What if Jocelyn sends me something? And what if Janelle reads it?"

I stayed quiet for a long second. Then I took the bottle from him and gulped down a swallow. After dealing with his drama, I was gonna have to check into AA.

Janelle

When I first heard the chime for the e-mail, I didn't really think anything of it. I had been fuming since David stormed out. I couldn't believe his reaction. I couldn't believe his questions. I couldn't believe his ass had the nerve to ask me, "Who?" He was lucky I had the baby inside of me because that's the only thing that kept me from slapping the shit out of him. Only for the sake of the baby did I hold things down.

I thought about my questions and accusations to him. And that's all they really were. There had been nothing behind them. They were empty—until he stormed out. That's when I realized he hadn't denied being with someone else.

I lifted my head from the arm of the sofa and glanced at the time. It was one-thirty in the morning. Who would be sending him mail at this time? I'd never looked at any of his personal things before because I never really felt like I had to. Plus, I respected his privacy, just like he did mine. But Tina's words popped into my mind.

"I bet his ass is writing . . . If your man ain't fucking you, he's fucking someone else."

I didn't want to believe it. I shook my head. And then I made my decision. I opened the laptop and stared at the name of the person who sent the e-mail. *Jocelyn?* I double-clicked on it and read the message:

David,

Hey sexy! I know it's one o'clock in the morning and you're probably sleeping, but I just couldn't get you off my mind, so I decided to say a quick hello. I also wanted to let you know how much I miss you! I didn't want to let you go, but I knew I had to. I keep thinking about that first weekend we had together. David, I can't wait to have your arms wrapped around me again. I feel so secure. And I have to say that making love to you is incredible. Only you could make me scream that way. Mmmmm . . . I want you even as I'm writing this!

Jocelyn

When I finished reading, I sat still with my hands trembling at my sides. I was in shock. I couldn't move. All of my suspicions had been confirmed.

"David is cheating on me." I whispered that over and over to myself.

My head began to throb at my temples, and my breathing became ragged. Then, rising up from deep within the pit of my stomach came a scream that seemed to go on forever.

David

I rushed home from Marc's with a sick feeling bubbling in the pit of my stomach. My luck was about to run out. I couldn't have been more right. I could feel it like the sweat dripping down the small of my back; I could feel it like the anxiety I felt when I laid my hand on the doorknob to my apartment.

It was a good thing that I had quick reflexes, or else I would never have been able to avoid the vase that was thrown at me when I opened the door.

Except for the shattering of glass, all I heard was Janelle screaming. "You lyin' motherfucker! You no-good, lyin'-ass motherfucker!"

Shit. I knew right away what had happened, but I had to play dumb. I braved her wrath and stepped inside and closed the door. "What the hell is wrong with you, Janelle? What the hell did you throw that at me for?"

She was relentless with her attack and threw another vase at me; this one still had roses in it.

I dodged it and flattened my back against the wall next to the door.

"You lyin' piece of shit! I read your fuckin' e-mail! I read *all* of them!"

"My e-mail?"

"Yes!" she shouted. "You dog-ass . . . pathetic-ass—" She picked up a bronze statue to throw next.

I threw my hands in the air. "Janelle, wait! Let's talk about this."

She hesitated and looked at me, her head tilted to the side, then threw the statue. It caught me in the side of my leg. "Go to hell!"

In the hallway outside, I could hear neighbors mumbling. Mrs. Newman from next door knocked on the door. "Is everything okay in there?"

"Yes," I said. The last thing I needed was for the neighbors to be in my business. "Everything's fine." I tried to sound as calm as I could.

"There you go, with your lyin' ass!" Janelle yelled out.

I had to do something. But what? She had every right to be angry with me. But still, I had to try something. It was either that or wait until she had nothing else to throw, and I didn't want to do that because we had some expensive shit.

I cautiously stepped toward her, making sure to keep my hands in the air. "Janelle, please, let's talk about this, baby. Please?"

"Don't *baby* me! Don't even go there with me."

I saw her eyes moving from left to right. I knew she was looking for something else to throw.

I quickly rushed toward her before she could think about throwing something sharp.

I regretted it instantly though, because after I took her in my arms, she began kicking and swinging and screaming even louder.

"Let me go, you lyin' bastard! Get your hands off of me!" She caught me in my shins twice and slapped me in my face.

I had to let her go.

More knocks came from the door.

Damn.

"Janelle, are you all right?" It was Mrs. Ortiz this time.

Damn. She loves to gossip, too.

"Everything's fine, Mrs. Ortiz," I yelled, wincing from the pain in my shins and the sting from the slap.

"Baby, please, let's just calm down and talk about this."

" 'Calm down'? You want me to calm down? You're fuckin' another woman. Were you calm when you fucked Jocelyn? Do you want me to read the e-mail to you? Do you want me to tell you how much she loved your first weekend together?"

I stayed silent and exhaled. I didn't know what to say. I stared at Janelle and saw the pain in her eyes, swollen from crying. I'd never felt more terrible.

Janelle fell to her knees, and instinctively, I moved toward her, but she held up her hand. "Unless you want your balls in your throat, you better not come near me."

I heeded her warning, like a good little boy. Silence reclaimed the room as fresh tears began to fall from her eyes. She was spent.

I moved to the sofa and sat down, closing my fists and pressing my knuckles together.

"I sent the bitch a message for you," Janelle said bitterly. "I told her she could have your ass, because I sure as hell don't want it."

"Can we please talk about this?"

"There's nothing to talk about."

"Janelle."

"Get out, David," she said softly.

"Janelle." I tried again.

"Get your pathetic ass out of this house!" she whispered.

"Please."

Janelle looked up at me with demon eyes. "Don't make me have to give birth to this baby behind bars."

I clenched down on my jaw and watched her as she fell forward and buried her face in her arms. I wanted to say something, anything to make things better. But what the hell could I say? The fact was, I fucked up royally.

Without a word, I stood up and stared at my laptop. I was surprised that she hadn't thrown that at me too. I grabbed it and walked through the rubble, but before I left I turned around. I watched Janelle crying softly and my heart ached. I never meant to cause her so much pain. I never meant to hurt her like that. I wanted to tell her that. But instead I opened the door and left.

As I stepped out into the hallway, our neighbors, the majority of whom were women, stared at me with accusatory glares. I walked past all of them silently to the elevator.

I didn't have to say a word, when Marc opened the door. All he had to do was look at me to know that I'd just come crashing down from the cloud I'd been on.

He stepped to the side to let me in and pointed to the couch. When I looked at it, I could only shake my head. He'd had a pillow and blanket waiting for me.

Jocelyn

Jocelyn,

I haven't heard from you all week. I hope that Janelle finding out about us hasn't scared you away. Please don't let it. This won't change anything between us. I want you to know that. I had been planning on telling her eventually anyway. I will admit, though, that I didn't want her to find out the way she did. It wasn't very pretty. But nevertheless, she did and now we can start spending as much time together as we had hoped. There are just a few loose ends that I need to tie up, so please bear with me. Right now, I'm staying at Marc's, but I will be getting my own apartment within the week. If I don't, Marc will kill me for cramping his style.

Anyway, please reply to this e-mail and let me know if you are okay with all of this. I don't want to lose you. Not again. And I know that you still have the situation with Eric to resolve, so I know that we can't rush anything. But I do want to make this happen.

Yours Always,
David

I could only sigh when I closed my e-mail. I wasn't trying to ignore or avoid David. I just needed some time to think. When I received the message from Janelle, I was in total shock. I could still see her words to me.

David is yours, bitch.

He was mine. All mine. That's what I wanted, wasn't it? I admit, I was happy. But a part of me felt incredibly sad for Janelle. I didn't know what I would have done in her shoes. I probably would have sent more than a message—maybe a bomb through the mail. I knew I wouldn't have been satisfied with just a reply.

Thinking about Janelle caused my thoughts to drift to Eric. How would he have handled the situation if he knew? Maybe he already did.

Since getting my number from Mari, he hadn't stopped calling. He kept leaving messages, begging for us to talk. It hurt so much to listen to the pain in his voice that I just started deleting the messages without listening to them.

He didn't deserve the treatment I was giving him. I knew that. And I knew that I needed to make some sort of a decision. I couldn't keep putting it or him on hold, especially now that David had moved out.

Everything was hinging on me now. But a divorce? I didn't know what to do. I loved David, there was no question, but I still cared for Eric. I had never expected the decision to be so hard.

To make matters worse, Mari and I had stopped talking. She refused to talk to me because of what I was doing. I knew that she wouldn't have been so angry if she didn't care, but still, she was acting like I was the worst person in the world. She was so busy worrying about how Eric felt and how he looked. Didn't she even take the time to consider my feelings? Couldn't she see that I was happy? The only thing she could say was that I had found a bedroom buddy. How could she?

And then she took it one step further and made it seem as if David didn't really care. How could she say that our relationship would fail? That hurt, and it pissed me off. I hung up on her after that.

I missed her, especially after Janelle e-mailed me, because I had no one else that I trusted to go to for advice.

David was all mine. But at what price?

David said he had to tie up a few loose ends. I did too. Without thinking, I reached for the phone and picked up the receiver. It didn't occur to me whose number I had dialed, until Eric answered the phone.

"Hello, Eric," I said in a whisper.

"Hello, Jocelyn."

I could hear the surprise in his voice. It had been a while since we had talked to each other. Hearing his voice made bumps rise from my skin.

"How are you?"

"I'm fine. How are you? I'm glad you called."

I remained silent and closed my eyes. My heart was beating so heavily that I felt short of breath. "Eric, can we meet somewhere and talk?"

When I hung up the phone, I sat silently and cried. I had made my decision, but it never occurred to me that the worst was yet to come.

Eric

I couldn't stop staring at her. She looked the same, yet so different. Something about her had changed. When I saw her number on the caller ID, I was so stunned that I almost didn't answer the phone.

For weeks I had been calling and leaving messages on her answering machine, begging for her to call me so that we could talk. That's all I wanted. It was painful to do, but I'd come to accept the reality that she'd considered our marriage over; I just wanted closure. I wanted to hear her tell me that it was.

And now I was sitting across from her. I looked at her left hand. The wedding ring wasn't there.

"So, how have you been?"

I think she saw that I noticed the ring was missing, because she pulled her hand away from the tabletop.

"I've been fine."

"How's the job?"

"The same. You?"

"They made me a partner last month. I'm the first and only black partner in the company's history."

"Congratulations."

"Thanks," I said with a half-smile.

When I was offered the position, I was ecstatic. I felt as though all my hard work and stressful nights had finally paid off. I called my family first. My father was proud and actually told me so, which made me feel good.

My parents wanted to have a small get-together for me the following weekend to celebrate. I didn't want them to because I knew I would've had to deal with questions about Jocelyn not being there, so I told them that she had to go away on business.

Unfortunately for me, they were going away on vacation, and they wanted to do it before their trip.

I reluctantly gave in.

The get-together was nice. Whenever anyone asked for Jocelyn, I just said that she wasn't home or she was away on a business trip. It was tough at first, but as the night went on, the lies became easier to cope with and give.

When I got home that evening though, everything came crashing down for me. It was then that reality set in for me.

I was alone.

The thought of not having Jocelyn in my life had never crossed my mind. All of a sudden, there in my empty home, my promotion didn't feel special anymore.

I tried to study her eyes to see if I could find something familiar within them, but she avoided my gaze. At that moment, I knew that I had the answer to my question.

"So, what did you want?" I just wanted to get it over with.

"Eric . . ." She looked away from the table and put her ringless hand to her face.

I sat stoic, as tears fell from her chin.

"Whoever he is, does he treat you the way you want to be treated?"

She shuddered and covered her face with both hands.

I sat and listened to her cry, and as I did, all I could think was how much I loved her. In a way, I blamed myself for bringing those tears upon her. If I had only loved her the way she needed to be loved, the way she wanted to be loved. I exhaled and lowered my head; I didn't know what else to say.

Finally, in a barely audible whisper, she said, "Yes."

Although I had braced myself for the blow, the pain I felt in my heart was still intense and excruciating. I fought to hold back my own painful tears. I didn't want her to see how much I was hurting. I pressed my lips together firmly and nodded. "I'm glad," I forced myself to say.

Jocelyn removed her hands from her face and looked at me. Her eyes were red and swollen. I reached out and gently wiped away a falling tear. It felt good to touch her skin again, even if it was only for a few seconds.

"I want you to be happy," I lied.

"I'm sorry, Eric. I never meant to . . . hurt you."

I shrugged my shoulders. "I'm sorry that my love wasn't enough."

She slowly rose from the table and reached into her pocket, a new wave of tears falling from her eyes. "I'm sorry," she whispered. In her hand she held the wedding ring.

I remained silent. What else could I have said?

"I'm sorry," she said again. She laid the ring down, grabbed her coat, and left.

I sat immobile and stared at what used to represent happiness.

I'll never forget the day I slipped it on her finger. That had been the happiest day of my life.

I painfully reached out and enveloped the ring in my hand. I was now at the opposite end of the spectrum.

Jocelyn

David moved in with me, and I couldn't have been any happier. It took four months, but we were finally able to be together openly. No more weekend rendezvous or e-mail exchanges. He was all mine, just like Janelle said.

After he moved his things in, the first thing we did together was go out and buy new furniture. (I gave the furniture I had to the Salvation Army.) We wanted the apartment to be a reflection of us. That was something that I never had with Eric. Nothing represented us. I decorated the house, because he'd always been too busy working and didn't have the time to devote toward our marriage. David wasn't like that.

The new furniture was his idea. "Let's decorate," he said. "Let's give this place our personality."

And that's what we did. We shopped until we got tired, buying a new living and dining room set. We bought a big-screen TV, a stereo, and new pots and pans. We wanted the entire place to say David and Jocelyn.

I couldn't help getting goose bumps when he was around me. He made me feel alive! And I know he felt the same because I could see the sparkle in his eyes and hear it in his voice. We were like kids back in high school again, enjoying every minute of it. It seemed as though our romance wouldn't die. We let our love bloom without boundaries. And just when I thought I had reached a level of happiness that I couldn't surpass, David always found a way to make my smile bigger.

Janelle

"Girl, I can't believe I just flew my ass over here. I must love your behind." Tina hugged me as best as she could then stepped back. "Damn, Janelle, you are huge! I know you're ready to drop that load."

"Girl," I said, wobbling beside her, *"ready* is not the word."

We both laughed as we headed to my car.

After David left, I fell into a state of mild depression. I cried, sulked, and cried some more. I didn't go to work for a week and ate just about every carton of cookies-n-cream I could get my hands on. That was my craving. I couldn't get enough.

On some nights, I woke up just to get a few spoonfuls. That eventually wore off, and with it, so did my depression. Actually, I just decided that I couldn't wallow in my self-pity anymore, because I had to be strong for my baby.

So I took the first step and called my parents to tell them the news. But for some reason, I didn't tell them why David and I ended the relationship. I just said that we'd been arguing too much and that it was better if we were apart.

I didn't tell them I was pregnant until the second time I

called, which was weeks later, because I didn't want to hit them with two bombs at once.

My mom took the news like any other mother usually does. She screamed and started thinking of names for the baby.

My father, being the man that he was, asked the all-important question. "Does David know?"

"Yes, he does."

"And what does he plan on doing?"

I wanted to say that his ass didn't have to do a damn thing, but instead I said, "He's going to be a father to his child." Even as I said that, I, too, wondered what his intentions were.

We had spoken only once since he'd left, and that had been just to arrange for him to come and pick up his things. Seeing him was hard. I didn't have to be there when he came; I didn't really know why I even bothered being there. We were like two strangers, as we barely said a word.

I was filled with so much anger and contempt that it had been a struggle to keep myself from throwing something else at him. When he left, the keys were lying on the coffee table.

I broke down later that night and called Tina. "He picked up his things today."

"About damn time," Tina said with her usual attitude. "He's lucky it wasn't me because I saw *Waiting to Exhale* and I would have been all Angela Bassett on his ass."

"What do I do now?" I asked.

I felt lost. David had been my right arm when I needed to punch; he was my right leg when I needed to walk. Nothing was the same without him. And with the baby coming . . .

"First of all, girl, you're gonna stop feelin' sorry for yourself, because none of this was your fault. That brother fucked up. It's better now than later anyway. Now you just need to put all your focus on you and your baby."

"I never thought I would be raising a baby alone."

"Girl, you are not on your own. You better realize that right away. You have your parents, you have your friends, and more importantly, you have me. What more do you need? Shit, just because a man is there don't mean that he's there anyway. You follow me?"

"I hear you. But it's still not easy."

"Shit, it's not supposed to be easy, girl. If it was, the world would be overpopulated with bastard children."

I had to laugh. Tina always had a unique perspective on life. I had to admit, her outlook helped to make things easier for me. That and the fact that we talked every week, sometimes every day, throughout my pregnancy.

With Tina's friendship and support, I got back my strength of self and began to realize that I really didn't need for David to be around. Hell, women raised children by themselves every day and with less than what I had. I was blessed to be in the position I was in.

I stopped letting David's absence bother me. He didn't have to call to see if the baby and I were all right. I guess he was too busy having fun with the new love of his life. I didn't know, but I didn't care anymore. I didn't need him, and I was happy. Happier than I'd been in a long time.

The prospect of motherhood really began to sink in for me around the seventh month, when the baby really started to kick. I didn't know if it was going to be a boy or a girl; I wanted to be surprised. But whichever it would be, he or she had some strong-ass legs.

In my eighth month, things really got tough. Sitting, walking, and even standing had become even more frustrating. Not to mention the major event called dressing. I had gained forty extra pounds and felt like a bloated whale. But as rough and uncomfortable as being pregnant was, I was still getting more and more excited and anxious about motherhood.

The only time I really got depressed was when I had to go

to my Lamaze classes alone. Seeing all of the women there with their husbands and boyfriends to help really got to me. They were constant reminders of the relationship that I used to have and the betrayal I was forced to endure.

Thankfully Tina was a phone call away to lift me up. I was grateful, when she offered to come to New York to help me down the home stretch of the term. Tina hated to fly. She couldn't even look at an airplane without becoming short of breath. I didn't really expect her to make the trip, until she called and told me what time to pick her up.

I opened the trunk for her to put her suitcase in then struggled to get behind the wheel.

"So, this is the Big Apple?" Tina asked with a sour face. "It should be called the Big *Clutter.*"

"Come on, Tina. LA is not that different."

"Maybe not, but at least in LA the people aren't in a rush to get into a traffic jam. Listen to these people. What the hell are they blowin' their horns for? Damn! They're not goin' anywhere."

I laughed out loud. It felt good to have her there.

"So, where are you takin' me to eat, big girl? You know I wasn't tryin' to eat on the plane."

"Take your pick—Italian, Southern, or Caribbean. I can't do Chinese. That'll make me throw up."

"I'm in New York, girl. Let's get some pizza."

Satisfying her wishes, we went and had some authentic New York pizza slices and a couple of Jamaican beef patties. As we ate, Tina made comment after hilarious comment about New Yorkers and their need to get everywhere in a hurry. I hadn't laughed so hard in a long time.

Raising a child alone was going to be tough, but I knew with friends like Tina, everything was going to be all right.

Marc

"Dave, my brother, you're my boy, you know that, right?" Dave looked at me with raised eyebrows. I knew that he could tell where I was headed. "Marc, man, we have gone over this before—"

I quickly cut him off. I didn't want to hear it. "Bruh, I've stayed quiet and watched you fuck around with Jocelyn these past couple of months like you didn't have shit else to worry about. But the fact is, *bruh,* you have a baby coming in another couple of weeks."

Dave put down his glass and turned on his stool to face me. "You don't need to remind me. I think about it every day."

"You could have fooled me, man."

"Just because I don't say anything doesn't mean I don't think about it. I lie awake at night thinking about it."

"Yeah, well you need to stop thinking and start doing. I'ma be straight up with you, man. The nothing that you have been doing is bullshit."

From the corner of my eye I could see Dave staring at me, but I didn't care. I had been quiet too long.

Before we met at the bar, I had stopped by Janelle's. It had been too long since we had talked. I knew I was to blame for that. Dave was my boy, and because I didn't want to betray him and our friendship, I betrayed Janelle instead. And that bothered me because she didn't deserve to be hurt. Dave may have played the fool, but I wasn't going to. I couldn't just ignore her. Besides, I was worried about her. So I stopped by to apologize and see how she and the baby were coming along. Her friend Tina was there, but she left us alone to talk.

I tried to stay away from the sore subject, when I was there, but Janelle didn't.

"Marc, what happened to David and me?"

I didn't know how to say that he fell in love with someone else. And even though she knew it, how could I say that? "I don't know."

"He hasn't come by, you know. He may not have feelings for me, but doesn't he care about his child?"

I watched the confusion in her eyes. "I've tried to talk to him, Janelle. But Dave's his own man. He'll do the right thing eventually. He may be a little slow, but he'll come around. Give him time. I know him."

Janelle smiled at me and held my hand. "Thanks for coming," she said. "I'm glad you did. I want you to know that I don't hold you responsible in any way for what happened. David is your friend, and I know you wouldn't betray him."

"Janelle, I'm sorry about all of this," I said sincerely. "I wish it wouldn't have happened. I really do."

"So do I. But things happen for a reason. I'll survive this. As far as David goes—fuck him. He doesn't have to come around." She squeezed my hand and then smiled. "Let's talk about something else."

I was fine with that. I felt so damn guilty. I mentioned the gym and the fact that I was thinking about opening a third one and putting it in Queens. She asked me about my relationship with Dahlia.

We talked for a good couple of hours. She sounded happy. I could hear excitement in her voice, when she talked about the baby, and that made me feel good.

I hated what Dave did to her. And really, it wasn't what he did that really got to me. It was how he did it. I mean, I'd dogged many women before too, so I didn't fault him for that. And it was cool that he and Jocelyn seemed to think they were each other's true love. I just didn't like how he threw Janelle to the side, especially after she told him she was pregnant. That bothered me the most.

He hadn't checked on her, hadn't checked on the baby. *Damn, I don't care how much the woman may hate me, the last thing I would do is neglect my responsibilities.* And that's exactly what Dave was doing.

"What the hell is bugging you, man?"

I could tell by the rise in his tone that he was getting pissed.

"Yo, you need to start acting like a man," I said bluntly. "You need to call Janelle and see how she and the baby are doing. And you need to tell Jocelyn what's going on."

"Janelle doesn't want to have anything to do with me."

"So? That doesn't mean that you can just forget about her. She was your fiancée. You fucked up and got caught. She has a right to be mad at you. But the last thing you should do is let her go through this alone. Damn, kid, at least let her know that you're going to take care of your child. Don't be a fucking deadbeat dad." I slammed my beer bottle on the countertop.

That was a sore subject for me because I'd seen too many of my other friends and family members neglect to take care of their kids. I never knew what the neglect was like personally because my father was always there for me, but I'd seen too many kids go astray because they weren't as lucky as I was. I knew Dave was better than he was showing. He was just scared, and I knew the only way for him to wake up was for me to shake him up a bit.

Dave lowered his head and sighed. "I never meant for any of this to happen. Shit, I didn't know things were going to go this far. Everything just kind of snowballed. One minute I was sending the e-mail, the next minute I'm making love to Jocelyn, and then Janelle's pregnant and screaming at me to get out of her life. Hurting her was the last thing I wanted to do."

"I know, bruh. But you played with fire. Someone had to get burned."

"I think about it every night. I lie awake and imagine holding my son or daughter in my arms. I've dreamt about it. I want to be a father."

"Then go to Janelle and let her know that. Shit, she may hate you for the rest of her life, but at least the kid will have a father. You don't want to let him or her grow up without one."

"Man, looking into Janelle's eyes hurt. She didn't deserve the pain."

I wanted to tell him that he was right, but I didn't want to make him feel any worse. I remained quiet and put my hand on his shoulder.

"You know what the worst part is?" he asked. He didn't wait for an answer. "The worst thing is, I don't even have the courage to tell Jocelyn. And I know that my cowardice may wipe out whatever happiness we're feeling."

"How can you be so sure?"

Dave lifted his head and looked at me. "Kid, I know Jocelyn. I'm sure."

"Then tell her," I said, ordering two more beers. "Why prolong it?"

"I'm too happy to do it."

" 'Too happy'?"

"Jocelyn is everything to me. These last couple of months have been perfect. I don't even know how to put into words how happy I've been. She makes me smile without doing anything at all. She makes me warm when I'm cold. I could make love to her every day for the rest of my life and feel like it's the first time. How could I possibly risk losing that?"

I handed him a Heineken and stared at him. I felt for him. I really did. It was tough to watch him go through the turmoil he was going through, but I didn't have any easy answers for him. I'd tried to warn him.

"You're about to become a dad, kid. You have no choice but to risk it."

Janelle

"**I** hate men!"

I was having contractions and dripping sweat as if I'd just stepped out of the shower. I'd never felt pain like that before. My contractions were minutes apart, and my back felt like it was being ripped in half. My hand was like a vise, clamped around Tina's hand. I couldn't let go. She tried to get me to use the breathing techniques they taught in the Lamaze classes, but I couldn't. Those techniques, and anything else I had learned, all went out the window. I just wanted to get it over with. Of course, I had no idea when that was going to be, because the baby didn't want to come out of me. I didn't know what it was going to be, but I promised myself that its first beating would be for all of the pain I was going through.

Another contraction came. I screamed and pushed at the same time. It was like not being able to go to the bathroom, but needing to so bad your insides were screaming.

"I hate men!" I yelled again.

Tina, who was enjoying my displeasure a little too much, laughed and caressed my forehead. "Of course you do, girl."

"I wish men had to give birth," I said angrily.

"Girl, if men had to give birth, we'd be using vibrators for the rest of our lives," Tina said in a you-know-men-ain't-shit tone.

I wanted to laugh, but screamed instead as another contraction came on.

The doctor instructed me to keep pushing.

"I can't," I said. I was drained and I could feel my body shutting down. I had no idea giving birth would be like this.

"Push, Janelle!" Tina coached, while wiping my forehead. "You can do it. Push that baby outta there. Come on, girl."

I squeezed my eyes, tightened my grip, and pushed with all I had left.

"I can see the head, Janelle," the doctor said excitedly. "That's it. Keep pushing!"

Tears leaked from my eyes. I felt faint and didn't know how much longer I could go on. I wanted it to be over.

"Another nice big push, Janelle," the doctor encouraged.

Tina stroked my hair and kissed my forehead. "It's almost over, girl. You can do it."

I was glad that she was there with me, but for a brief moment, I wished David was.

We had always talked about having children. He wanted a boy, and I wanted a girl. I thought he was going to be a good father. *Bastard.*

I screamed out one last time, and this time, when my scream was over, so was the pain.

I opened my eyes and watched as the doctor stood up.

"It's a healthy baby boy!"

I leaned my head back on the pillow, while Tina continued to stroke my hair. A boy. I closed my eyes then, and in the darkness I saw David smile. "Bastard," I whispered. Then the exhaustion claimed me, and I passed out.

* * *

When I woke up, the first thing I saw was Tina smiling at me from a chair against the wall. "Girl, it's about time," she said, rising from the seat.

"What time is it?"

"It's twelve in the afternoon. You fell right out after you delivered."

My baby! I felt my stomach. Sure enough, it wasn't a dream. "Where is he?"

"He's in the nursery. Are you ready for him?"

I smiled. "Yes!"

Tina squeezed my shoulder and walked out of the room, leaving me alone.

I took that time to reflect on the new adventure that I was about to begin. I was now a single mother. And scared. Tons of questions popped into my mind. What if I didn't raise him properly? What if he grew up thinking he didn't have enough love? Or too much? What would I tell him about girls? What if he grew up and was gay? What then? Should I spank him or give him time-outs? What time should I send him to bed? Who would watch him when I had to work? What about when he became sick? On and on they came, like a barrage of bullets that I couldn't avoid.

"The nurse will bring him in a few minutes," Tina said, walking back into the room.

A few minutes later, the nurse, who resembled a heavier version of Alice from *The Brady Bunch,* sauntered in with my son. She checked his ID bracelet and then checked mine. "Yup," she said with a smile. "He's yours. Are you ready for him?"

I could only nod my head and sit upright. My heart was dancing, and my fingers were shaking.

"Here he is," she said, resting him into my arms. "All six pounds, seven ounces of him."

I looked down at him and immediately started to cry. In my arms, I held the most beautiful little boy—my son.

"He's going to have your eyes. I can tell," Tina said quietly.

He opened them briefly and then shut them. He still wasn't used to the light. "Hey, little man," I whispered, touching his tiny nose. "I'm your mommy."

He moved for a moment and then fell still.

I stroked his head, which was full of curly black hair like his father's. I couldn't stop crying. I was on cloud nine. "I'm your mommy," I said again and caressed his soft baby skin. He was pale, but I knew that his color hadn't set in yet. He looked like a wrinkled little man.

"So," Tina said, standing over me, "what's his name, girl?"

"Name?"

I had labored over this for the past couple of months. I had a girl's name, but I had never been able to decide on one for a boy. I knew that I wanted him to have my father's name in the middle, but I had no idea what I wanted to name him.

I kissed his forehead and looked into his puffy eyes. And then, just like magic, it came.

"Isaiah Joseph." I held Isaiah closer to me and kissed his forehead. I knew that I was going to be the best mother possible. I continued to cry; for the first time in months, I wasn't mad at David.

Tina stayed with me for another month.

My parents, who had missed the delivery because of bad weather, had to fly in the day after and left two weeks later to go back home. Before my father had gotten on the plane, he told me to tell David congratulations. They still had no clue about what had really happened between us. When they asked why he wasn't there with Isaiah and me, I told them that he had an unavoidable business trip and had to leave right after the birth.

I still couldn't tell them the truth. I couldn't tell them that he hadn't seen Isaiah.

Tina didn't agree with me. "Girl, you're gonna have to tell them sooner or later. You might as well get it over with."

"I can't right now. I'm not ready to deal with that yet." And I wasn't. I was too happy to go backwards. And that's just how I looked at it—David was the past, and Isaiah was my future.

Tina sucked her teeth. "Whatever, girl."

I was grateful for all of the help from everyone, but I owed her the biggest debt of gratitude. She put her life on hold to help get me through the most difficult thing I'd ever had to face. She was the angel I needed, when I asked God what I was going to do. I was sad to see her leave. It made me really miss being back home and having that support close by.

I was still exhausted and wasn't fully healed, but little by little, I did more each day.

I sat heavily in my sofa and looked around. The place was disheveled. In the kitchen, dishes needed to be washed and put away. In the living room, furniture had been moved to the side to allow room for Isaiah's playpen and walker—a premature gift from Mrs. Newman next door. He wasn't quite ready for all of that.

People came out of the woodwork to offer me gifts and flowers after Isaiah's birth. I'd received everything from a crib and stroller to bottles and leak-proof diapers. I didn't have to buy anything.

My first night alone with Isaiah was scary and quiet. Of course, I wasn't going to complain. I closed my eyes and exhaled a long sigh of relief. Isaiah was in his bassinet sleeping soundlessly. I stretched my arms and legs. I had no idea that caring for a baby was so much work. I was a slave as I breastfed every two hours, changed his diapers every hour, and held him in my arms and rocked him all day long just to keep him from crying. I gained a newfound respect for my mother—hell, all mothers for that matter.

I stood up and listened to the silence around me. It was

unnerving. I'd become used to hearing Tina's loud-ass laughter and my mother's constant cooing over Isaiah. Even my father had gotten the fits. I wasn't daddy's little girl while he was here. It was all about Isaiah Joseph. My son.

I went to the bassinet and watched him sleep. He was so innocent, happy and precious. He seemed to smile in his sleep. What was I going to tell him about his father? Perhaps a better question was, did his father even care? I'm sure he knew about Isaiah's birth, because Marc had come to visit us. (It was nice seeing him again.) He brought Isaiah a Scooby-Doo stuffed animal, and me a "Best Mommy" T-shirt and a bouquet of roses. I was grateful for his visit. No matter what happened between David and me, it was comforting to know that Uncle Marc would always be there for me. I was sure that he told David about his son.

I tiptoed away from my angel and went into the bedroom. It was no less chaotic. Cleaning was the one thing that I didn't have time for. The mess reminded me of David. Damn it, I missed him. I tried not to, but I found it impossible.

I thought about when I went off on him after reading the e-mail. I hated him. I wanted to hurt him so badly. I sat on the edge of my bed and did something I said I wouldn't do. I wondered what I had done wrong. What was it that I hadn't given him that he was getting from Jocelyn? I wanted to hate her too, but I couldn't. The harsh reality was that something had gone wrong with David and me, and she was obviously there to set it right for him. I lay back on the bed and hugged my pillow in my arms. I fell asleep, blaming myself for all that had happened.

I woke up two hours later to the sounds of Isaiah's cry. It was feeding time.

David

I never thought that I would be lying to Jocelyn, but I couldn't tell her what I was going to do. After Marc told me about Isaiah's birth, my world just seemed to rotate off of its axis. I had a son and I hadn't been there. Damn. Marc told me how he had gone by a few times to see Janelle and the baby. He described how cute he was and how much he looked like me. I put on a smile when he described Isaiah Joseph in detail. I think he did that on purpose to really get to me. It worked.

When we got off the phone, I sat silent for what seemed like hours. I couldn't believe that I had missed my own son's birth. I couldn't believe that I had missed the first two months of his existence. My son. My Isaiah. I had to see him.

When I called and told Marc what I planned on doing, he said, "It's about damn time, bruh."

"Yeah . . ."

"You ready to tell Jocelyn?"

"No. I can't tell her the truth yet. I'll tell her I'm going away for the weekend for business."

"Dave—"

"Not yet, man."

I still couldn't tell her the news. It was probably good for us anyway, because things weren't the same. I had changed. My mind had been occupied by Isaiah day in and day out. I had dreamt of seeing him take his first baby steps. I daydreamed about taking him to the park and teaching him how to play basketball and football. Why was I risking missing out on all of that? That question led to only one answer—I had to see him.

Jocelyn

D avid had to go away for the weekend for a book signing. I can't say that I wasn't happy about it. I think we needed the space. I know I did. For several months he had been acting weird. He seemed to be somewhere else other than where he was. It was worrying me. We seemed to be doing less and less each day. We were falling into a rut. I would work all day and come home in desperate need for some affection. But being a writer, it seemed as if he was always working. He was always in front of his laptop, typing away furiously.

Some nights, I tried to stay up and wait until he finished, but most of the time I fell asleep alone. I began to wonder if he was regretting being with me. The kisses weren't the same anymore. His hugs weren't as strong. They say absence makes the heart grow fonder. Hopefully the weekend would prove that to be true, because things had to change and change fast.

I tried to call Mari again, but all I got was her answering machine. I left another message for her. I missed my sister. We'd never had anything come between us like this before.

Throughout my entire life, whenever I needed a shoulder

to cry on, she had been there. It worked the same way when she needed me to help deal with the physical abuse. We were each other's rocks. And I needed her. But how mad was she? I went by her job a few times, but each time I did, she was never there. I was lonely, even when David was home.

From time to time I would think about Eric. I couldn't get the last moment I said good-bye to him out of my mind. His demeanor was so impassive, and from the questions he asked me, he knew that it was over between us. I felt horrible. Giving the ring back had been one of the hardest things I'd ever had to do. I think what hurt the most was the lack of emotion he showed when I laid it on the table. He hadn't even reached for it.

I'll never forget how nervous he was when he proposed to me. He could barely look me straight in the eye. I promised him that night that I would love him forever. I wonder how much he hated me when I reneged on my vow.

I picked up the phone to call Mari again, just to see if my luck had changed. When her answering machine came on, I hung up. I turned on the TV to find something to keep me company, and as *Friends* did their best to cheer me up, I suddenly had a bad feeling that I couldn't shake.

Janelle

When I heard the knock on the door, I had just finally been able to sit my behind down for a break, after struggling to get Isaiah to fall asleep. He had been fighting sleep like a champ and refused to go down without a fight. Usually I could wind up the Sesame Street mobile hanging above his crib and he would watch it spin around until his eyes closed, but this time he wasn't having it. He cried and screamed so much it had me worried. I couldn't figure out why he wouldn't go to sleep, even though I could see in his eyes that he was bone-tired.

I gave him several Mylecon drops for gas, hoping that would work, and when it didn't, I called my mother. She laughed and recounted to me how I used to do the same thing when I was an infant, and people used to think I was being abused.

"Just rock him and hum a tune until he gives in, child. He'll be all right. Babies do that sometimes."

I took her advice and, even though I couldn't sing to save my life, I sang and hummed the hell out of "Rockabye Baby" until, just like my mother said, he fell off to dreamland. I had to do that several times, because each time he fell asleep and I put him down in his crib, he'd wake up and start screaming again. Finally, after a third time, I was able to breathe a sigh of relief, when I laid him down and he remained sleeping.

I groaned as I got up from the couch and went to the door. I checked the peephole. My heart skipped a beat as I stared at a ghost from the past. I opened the door. "What are you doing here?"

"Hello to you too, Janelle," David said.

I slit my eyes at him. "I asked you a question. What are you doing here?" I spread my arms apart in the doorway to let him know that he wasn't welcome.

"I came to see my son."

I had to laugh. "Your son? That's a joke. Why don't you do what you do best and disappear? *My* son doesn't need to see you."

"Please. Let me see him, Jocelyn."

I stood still and didn't answer him right away. I could tell by the determined look in his eyes that getting him to leave wasn't going to be easy. And I couldn't honestly say that I wanted him to go. As angry as I was at him, and as much as I hated what he did, my love for him had not entirely gone away. He had captured my heart in a way that no other man had before, and I would have been lying if I said that I didn't feel anything for him still. But I wasn't about to let him know that.

"You have some nerve calling him your son."

"Janelle . . . I . . ."

"Don't say a damn word. You weren't concerned about him when he was in my stomach, and you sure weren't concerned when he was born. So why are you worried about him now?" I held my ground and glared at him.

"Look," he said softly, "you have every right to be angry with me, okay. I have been a bastard. I know that. But you don't know the things that have been going through my mind. It hasn't been as easy for me as you think."

"Things going through your mind? You're so full of shit! If you gave a shit, you would've had the decency to call once in a while to make sure everything was fine. *If* your son mattered, you would've been there for his birth. I know you knew when he was born because I'm sure Marc, who's come by more than once, told you. But instead of worrying, you were too busy trouncing around with your bitch! Isn't that right?"

"Look, there's not a whole lot I can say, Janelle. I didn't come here to argue. I just want to see him. And I need to explain some things to you. I want him *and* you to know that he has a father."

"Spare me your explanations, please. Better yet, spare him. He's been fine up 'til now. He doesn't need a father like you." Before he could say another word, I slammed the door hard in his face and locked it.

From the other side, David banged on the door and called out to me. "Janelle, please. Just let me see him!"

"Go away!" I started to cry as he continued his assault on the door. "He doesn't need you!"

"Let me see him, please? Don't turn me away."

I shivered against the door as tears fell from my chin to the floor. I could hear Isaiah starting to cry again. "Go away, David!"

Noises flooded in all around me—David, Isaiah, myself—I wanted to scream.

As Isaiah's screaming grew in volume, David's banging became more insistent.

"Please," I whispered. "Just leave us alone."

But I didn't want him to. Even though he had caused me

unforgivable pain, I wanted my child to have a father. And until he showed up, I didn't think that was going to happen. Amidst Isaiah's cries and David's pleas, I unlocked the door. "Your son is crying," I said without emotion. I turned away from him and went back to the couch.

David walked inside and said, "Thank you." Then he went back to the bedroom. When Isaiah's crying ceased, I thought about how unfair life was.

David

I never knew the magnitude of power a child wielded, until I held Isaiah in my arms. Bumps rose from my skin when he stopped crying and looked at me. Up until that moment, I had never felt more important or necessary. My life ceased being my own as I rocked him back and forth. I couldn't stop looking at him. He had my nose, and even at three months old, his eyes were as intense as Janelle's.

He made tiny sounds as I kissed him continuously on the top of his head, which was full with my hair. With his head against my shoulder, I realized how shameful it had been to miss out on a truly amazing experience—his birth.

"I'm sorry for not being there," I whispered.

I admit I was surprised by my behavior. The last thing I had expected was to be standing still with tears in my eyes and the absolute desire to protect. I'd been a fool. I kissed his forehead and swallowed his hand in mine. "I'm sorry," I whispered again, closing my fingers around his. "I love you. Do you hear me, Isaiah? Your daddy loves you."

"He recognizes you," I suddenly heard Janelle say from behind me.

I kept my back to her. I couldn't bring myself to look at her. I was too ashamed. "You think so?"

"Oh, he knows who you are. Just look at him. Look at his eyes. They may look like mine, but he speaks with them just like you do."

I kissed his forehead again and then laid him back down in his crib. He stared at me with an infectious smile. Tears from my eyes fell onto the mattress. Isaiah squirmed and made a soft baby sound.

"What do you think he's saying?" I asked, caressing his skin.

"Where the hell you been?" Janelle answered with heavy attitude.

I bent down and kissed his forehead, then his hands and feet. "I'm here, little man," I said, my heart filled with regret.

He smiled again, exposing tiny dimples, and moved his hands and feet.

I smiled too and then stood upright, but I didn't turn to face Janelle. I didn't know what to say. I stood mute and looked at the Scooby-Doo border above the crib. Janelle had always liked that cartoon. I guess Isaiah eventually would too. The rest of the wall was painted in blue, with basketball, baseball, and football clouds.

"You've done a great job with him," I said, staring at a picture of them on a nightstand next to the crib. "A really great job."

"I had help. Tina came and stayed with me during the last couple of weeks of my term then stayed for a month more after I delivered. My parents were here also."

"How are they?" I had become very close to them over the years. Betraying Janelle was like betraying them too.

"They're fine. My father said to tell you, 'Congratulations.'"

"'Congratulations'?"

"I told them we broke up because we had been arguing all the time. I didn't tell them what really happened between us. I also told them you had to leave for business right after he was born. They don't know anything."

"Thank you," I said, appreciative of her discretion.

"*Don't* thank me," she snapped. "I had enough shit to deal with. The last thing I needed was to answer all of the questions they asked."

I finally turned around and looked at her. She looked the same, with the exception of a few additional baby pounds around her midsection and hips, and her hair was no longer shoulder-length, but hung just above her chin in layers. The new style worked well on her, but then she always had been able to pull off any style.

"I like your hair," I said honestly.

"I cut it today. I needed a change," she said, sending a clear message with her direct tone.

"It looks good."

She nodded. Then we stared at each other without exchanging a word. It was awkward, and I was nervous. There were so many things I had planned on saying, but right then and there, I just couldn't seem to make the words come out.

"You need to leave, David," Janelle finally said, walking out of the bedroom.

I turned and looked once more at my son, who'd fallen asleep. I touched his forehead gently. "I'll be back, little man." I kissed him again and then left the room.

"Janelle," I said, stepping into the living room I used to know so well, "there are some things I need to say to you."

"You have nothing to say to me. At least nothing that I want to hear."

"Janelle, please?" I implored softly.

"What? What do you have to say that you haven't already? Oh wait, you never actually said anything. I just happened to catch your ass."

"I'm sorry."

"'Sorry'? Tell me something, David—how long would you

have gone on being 'sorry,' with Jocelyn on the side? Bitch. Is she sorry too?".

"Jocelyn has nothing to do with this."

Janelle's eyes widened with disbelief. " 'Nothing to do with this'? Oh, I think she has everything to do with this. How dare you stand there and defend her to me?"

"Janelle, I know that I hurt you."

"You didn't just hurt me," Janelle screamed, cutting me off. "You broke my heart. You had it in the palm of your hand and you used that to your advantage to play me for a fool. Just tell me one thing—why? Why did you do it? Why did you do that to us?"

I pressed my lips together and breathed in deeply. I wanted to leave so badly. I began to think that going there was a mistake, but I knew better, because I saw how much my son needed me and how much I needed him. Besides, I deserved everything Janelle was giving me, and more. I exhaled. "Our love just died," I said as honestly as I could.

"Bullshit! Don't you dare speak for the both of us."

"Well, what do you want me to say, Janelle?" I asked, frustration setting in.

"Just be a man, David!" Janelle yelled out. "You were man enough to cheat, so be a fucking man now!"

"And say what?" I said, louder than I had intended. I could feel the argument coming. I should've walked out the door without another word. But like a fool, I didn't. "What could I possibly say that would make you feel better?"

"Go to hell!"

"Do you want to hear that I was the one that fell out of love? Do you really want to know that I wasn't happy anymore? Does knowing that make you feel better?"

She stood in front of me, tears snaking from the corners of her eyes. I hated seeing her that way. She was innocent, and I knew that. Why didn't I just leave?

"You're a goddamned bastard, you know that?"

"Finally, we agree."

"Get out, David," Janelle said, her tone filled with disgust. "Get the hell out now!"

"Or what? You'll throw something at me again?"

"Yes!"

"Damn it, Janelle! I didn't come here to argue with you. That's the last thing that we need to be doing. Honestly, I think that you need to come to terms with the reality of our situation. Our relationship is over. But that is my son in there, whether you like it or not. And I'm going to take care of him. So we're going to have to find a way to get past all of this and be civil toward each other."

As we stood there staring at one another, Isaiah began to cry again. I looked toward the bedroom.

"Get your ass out of my house now, David," she said, pushing past me and going to the bedroom.

When she came back, Isaiah was in her arms, sniffling. He looked at me and I looked at him.

"I'm sorry for ever hurting you, Janelle," I said, looking at her. "I know that you didn't deserve any of it."

Janelle didn't say anything. She walked past me to the door and opened it. "For the last time, leave!" she demanded.

I walked to the door and looked again at my son. I tried to give him a kiss goodbye, but Janelle turned him away from me.

"I'll be back, little man," I said softly. I had barely been an inch out of the doorway, when the door slammed behind me. I leaned against the door and bowed my head.

Janelle and I used to be so happy together. She was my best friend, and I was hers. We always wanted children. I once told her that I would die for her.

I lifted my head and sighed. "I'll be back, little man," I said again, walking away.

* * *

A month passed before I saw Isaiah again, and when I did, once again Janelle and I had it out. We couldn't avoid an argument. Even though I'd found ways to come to New York and see him consistently for several weeks—something Janelle agreed to—her anger never seemed to subside. No matter what I said or did, she just couldn't seem to avoid reminding me of what I had done. I didn't want to argue with her, but her constant reminders, plus the fact that I knew I was digging one hell of a hole for myself because I still hadn't told Jocelyn about Isaiah, would just get to me and I'd flip out and we'd go at it.

I was stressed.

I couldn't write.

Janelle wouldn't ease up.

Jocelyn was completely in the dark.

That was the kicker. I kept waiting for the right time to tell Jocelyn about Isaiah, but it just seemed that there was never a right time. As happy as we were, the addition of Isaiah into my life had really caused things to change between us. Because his existence was a secret, it was necessary for me to leave periodically to see him, which meant that I had to come up with different lies, and that was putting a strain on me and us.

We began to argue about little things—things that we shouldn't have cared about. And to top it off, when I was home, I was engrossed in my laptop, trying to complete my novel, which I was hating more and more as I wrote it.

That only created more frustration for me and more distance between us. But I couldn't help it. I was already behind schedule. My agent was pissed, and I couldn't blame her. I had written two hits in a row, and she wanted more. Hell, I did too. I just couldn't focus.

But not everything was going down the drain. Our sex life didn't change. We still had sex like teenagers who'd discovered it for the first time and couldn't get enough. But good sex alone couldn't sustain us.

I was being split in two different directions. I had Jocelyn and whatever our relationship was at one end and my son at the other. The worst part of it all was that my cowardice was keeping me from being the kind of father I wanted to be. All because I couldn't tell Jocelyn.

"Marc, man, what the hell should I do?" I couldn't believe I had gotten myself into the predicament I was in. I curled the dumbbell and grunted out loud.

"Bruh, you already know what I think," Marc said, as he did his own set beside me.

Since I had moved from New York to Maryland, working out had been one thing I'd barely done. This was my first workout in a while, and I was rusty. I'd come to spend the weekend with my boy, but I'd also come to see my son.

"But if I do that," I said, struggling with a usually light fifty-pound dumbbell, "Jocelyn and I are done."

"Maybe she's stronger than you think, man. Maybe she'll understand."

I let the weight drop and wiped sweat from my forehead. "I told you before, there's no chance in hell she'll be down with that."

"She might have been if you would've said something when this all happened."

I frowned and grabbed the weight and did another set of curls, just out of frustration. Marc was right. He had always been right. Shit.

"What the hell have I gotten myself into?" I said, dropping the weight again.

"A web, bruh."

"Yeah, and no matter which way I move, it's going to rip."

"Well, then ask yourself this—which side of the web is more important to you?"

The next morning, before I drove back to Maryland, I stopped by Janelle's to see Isaiah again. I bought him a stuffed Elmo, and Janelle a bouquet of flowers as a peace offering. I didn't want to argue with her. I was glad when she accepted the flowers without a word.

I played with Isaiah for a long while. At the rate he was growing, I figured he would be ready to join the NBA by the time he hit fifteen. It was hard to believe that he had been born just six months ago. Saying good-bye to him was getting harder and harder to do.

During my drive home, I couldn't help but think about Marc's question. What was more important? My relationship with my son or my love affair with Jocelyn?

David

I'd never truly been scared in my life before, until the night Janelle called me while Jocelyn and I were sitting down to eat dinner by candlelight.

"Don't answer it," I said.

I had surprised her by preparing dinner and having candles lit when she came home. It was my attempt at changing the tide of our relationship, which was fizzling more and more each day. I was also trying to make things more solid between us before I told her about Isaiah. He was growing, and with it, my responsibilities were too. I could no longer be a once- or twice-a-month father.

It took four months, but my relationship with Janelle was getting better. We didn't argue every time we saw each other, and if we did, it had to do with Isaiah, which was okay with me. It showed that he had loving parents. I had even spent some nights on the couch by her—drama-free.

Janelle was a great mother. She did everything and anything to keep our son smiling. She also wasn't seeing anyone, which, I must admit, I was kind of happy about because the idea of another man being around my son didn't sit well with me at all. But I knew her being single wasn't going to be a permanent thing. Another brother was bound to come along because let's face it, Janelle was a beautiful, intelligent, and strong black woman. When that happened, I knew my stopping by whenever I wanted to was going to have to stop. That's why I started considering filing for joint custody.

But I still had to discuss my feelings with Janelle, and doing that meant I had to tell Jocelyn about Isaiah. I was still in the web, but at least I knew which way I needed to squirm to get out of it. I just had to damn the consequences of the tearing on the other side.

I was in the first stages of *Project Prep Jocelyn,* when the phone call came.

Jocelyn stood up from the table. "I have to get it. It could be work."

"Let work go to the answering machine."

"Just one call. I promise," she said with a sexy smile.

"Get rid of them quickly."

She winked at me and went to get the phone.

I sat at the table, thinking about my life. I had a woman that I loved and a beautiful son. I prayed that Jocelyn would be able to accept him.

She quickly came back to the table, phone in her hand. "It's for you," she said. Her face no longer held the smile, but wore a mask of puzzlement.

"For me? Who is it?"

"It's Janelle," she said, her voice low and tone irritated.

I stared at her to see if she was joking, but by the dim in her usually sparkling brown eyes, I knew that she wasn't. I got up took the phone. "Janelle?" I said cautiously. *Why didn't she call my cell phone?*

"David!" Janelle screamed frantically.

I knew something was wrong immediately. "What's wrong?"

"Isaiah . . . he . . . he started wheezing. His skin . . . it . . . it . . ." she paused, which made my heart beat even faster than it already was.

"What about his skin, Janelle?" I asked nervously. "What's wrong with his skin?"

Janelle was crying. "It became so pale," she struggled to get out. "He . . . he wouldn't respond to me."

"Try to calm down, Janelle," I said, struggling to do that myself. I sat down, while Jocelyn watched me with confusion and contempt. *Shit.*

I turned my back to her. "Just try to stay calm, Janelle, please, and tell me what's happened."

Janelle sniffed and with her throat choking with tears, said, "About an hour ago I noticed that Isaiah's breathing wasn't right. I tried . . . tried to put some Vick's on his chest to see if that would help. But. . . . but he only got worse. He was wheezing so loudly. David, I'm scared. He sounded so terrible."

As Janelle cried harder, I squeezed my temples. "Try to stay calm, Janelle," I said again. I was on the brink of losing control myself, but I knew I couldn't do that. "Where are you now?"

"We're at the hospital. Marc drove us over."

"Everything's going to be all right," I said, praying it would be. "You have to believe that, okay. Just try to relax. The doctors will help him. What hospital are you in?"

As Janelle gave me the hospital name, my hands wouldn't stop shaking. I had to force myself to breathe calmly. I had to remember to take my own advice.

When I hung up the phone, I closed my eyes and then opened them, only to see Jocelyn glaring at me with heavy accusation.

Shit. The time had come. I refused to look away. "I have to leave for New York right away. My son is in the hospital."

I must have called Janelle's cell phone at least two thousand times on my way to New York, but she didn't answer. I was getting more and more worried. Even though I had my radio on, the only thing I could hear was the fear in her voice. Once or twice, I tried to drown out the noise by turning up my radio full blast, but it didn't work. Besides, I needed to be able to hear my phone if she called. Damn.

I was driving at an average of ninety miles an hour, but I wasn't worried about a speeding ticket. I had to get to Isaiah's side. Damn the distance. I looked at my watch. I still had a couple more hours to go.

I had to know something. I dialed Marc's number but got his voice mail. Shit. For the longest time, I felt like I was standing at the bottom of a hill, looking up at the ball of life as it careened on the edge, threatening to tumble toward me. Well, now it had tumbled and grown in size, and there was no way for me to avoid its path.

Janelle and I.

Isaiah's health.

Jocelyn.

Damn.

Jocelyn. I still didn't know what to make of her reaction, when I told her the news about Isaiah. She didn't really give one, and that had me worried. I think I would have felt better if she went off on me and threw something. I was used to that. I could have handled some screaming, but I didn't get any of that either. She just sat as still and quiet as a statue. I couldn't read her. She didn't say a word, when I got dressed, slipped on my coat, or when I grabbed my keys and headed toward the door.

I hesitated before I left, hoping that she would say something. I even called out her name, but the only answer I received was silence. Damn, I hated the unknown. I had no idea what to expect when I got back home. And the bad thing about it all was that I had brought this all on myself.

Responsibilities

Janelle

After I called David, I hurried back to be with Isaiah. The doctor had him hooked up to a breathing machine, which was creating a medicated mist for him to breathe through a facemask. His stomach was moving up and down so deep and so fast. His skin color was still pale. I felt so helpless.

"When will his breathing return to normal?" I asked the doctor working on him. "And why is he still pale?"

"Ms. Atkins, we have to give the medication some time to work. He's had a very serious asthma attack. You'll have to be patient."

"But he's going to get better, right? Once the medication works, Isaiah will be fine, right, doctor?"

"Let's hope so. I promise, we'll do all we can to make that happen."

I moved away from him and went back by Isaiah's side. Teardrops fell from my eyes as I watched him struggle to breathe. He looked so much smaller, hooked up to the machine. I caressed his tiny arm.

"Breathe for me, little man. You can do it. Take a big

breath for Mommy." My hands shook terribly. I said a silent prayer and took hold of his hand.

Although Marc and Dahlia had come to the hospital with me and were in the waiting room, I still felt like I was alone. I missed having David there. He had always been my rock, whenever a crisis came up, and I truly needed his strength and stability then. Calling him hadn't been a hard decision. He may have been an ass in the beginning, but as time passed, he had worked to make up for his not being there.

Just as I always knew he would be, David was a good father. He was attentive and genuine and did whatever he had to do to see his son smile. Watching him with Isaiah always made me smile. The times when all three of us were together were special and felt right. Sometimes I found myself daydreaming about us being a family. But then David would announce it was time for him to leave, and I'd snap back into reality.

I had to applaud Jocelyn for dealing with the situation the way she was. I always wondered what the moment had been like, when he told her I was pregnant. How had she taken it? I'll be honest, I wanted it to hurt. I wanted her to feel pain just like I did.

When she answered the phone, I almost hung up on her. David had given me his home number in case of an emergency. I never planned to use it, because I never wanted to hear her voice, but when he didn't answer his cell, I had no choice. It took me a second to speak when Jocelyn answered the phone. I'll admit, for a split second, I thought about hanging up, because the last person I ever wanted to talk to was that bitch. But like her or not, my son came first.

There was still another couple of hours left before David would reach New York. I prayed that all would go well and I'd be at home, breathing a sigh of relief, when he did.

I continued to caress Isaiah's arm and watch his chest rise and fall. Asthma. David had asthma in his family. Now, I did too. Isaiah's breathing seemed to be calming down.

"That's right, little man," I said softly. "Breathe for Mommy." I allowed myself to relax one notch.

"Looks like the medicine is working," the doctor said, walking in and checking Isaiah's breathing.

"Thankfully."

"How about some coffee?"

"I could use some."

"There's a machine at the end of the hall. Why don't we get some and let Isaiah rest for a while."

I needed the boost, but I didn't want to leave. "I should stay at his side."

"We'll be right back."

I turned and stared at my son. It somehow seemed like a cruel punishment to have him hooked up to the machine the way he was. I wanted to take his place.

"I'll be right back, baby."

As the doctor and I walked, I took a few deep breaths.

"Scared you, huh?"

I looked at his name badge for the first time. "Doctor Chin, *scared* is not the word. How did this happen?"

"Well," he said, sliding coins into the coffee machine, "it's tough to say what causes asthma to develop. The most common cause is a respiratory virus. Both children and adults experience respiratory infections, but children, especially infants, are more susceptible. Is there a history of asthma in your family?"

"Not in mine, but his father's, yes."

"Well, Isaiah should be at home and back to normal by the time he gets here."

"That'll be a relief. What are the chances of this happening again?"

"It's almost impossible to predict. There are many things that can cause an attack—pollen, dust, strenuous activity; there's no real way of knowing, with asthma. My youngest son has it, but it only bothers him in the summertime. My

oldest son had it but grew out of it, and my daughter never
had it. But my sister's little girl has it so severe, she can barely
take a walk around block. It's a tough thing to predict. But
when it happens, you just do the best you can to get it under
control."

"I thought I was going to lose him," I said, sipping on the
coffee.

"The first episode is rough. But like anything, you learn to
cope and manage it."

I smiled and felt somewhat comforted by his words. I knew
that I wasn't going to feel better, though, until Isaiah was out
of the hospital. But still, his reassurance was nice to have.

"I should probably go out to the waiting area and tell my
friends the news. Then they can stop worrying."

"That would be a good idea."

"Would you mind coming with me? They may have some
questions I haven't thought of."

"Sure."

When Doctor Chin and I walked into the waiting room,
Marc looked up from a magazine he had been reading and
stood up to meet me. "Is Isaiah okay?" he asked with worried
eyes.

"He's fine," I said with a half-smile. "He had an asthma attack. This is Doctor Chin."

Marc shook the doctor's hand and then looked at me.
"How are you holding up?"

"I'm fine. Just a little shaken up."

"Once we are confident that Isaiah's breathing is back to
normal, we'll let you all go home."

Marc smiled at me and took my hand in his then turned
to Dahlia, who had been with him that evening. I'd met her
months before when Marc came to drop off a gift for Isaiah.
I hadn't really had a chance to talk to her for too long, but
for the length of time that I did, I knew that she was right for
Marc. Unlike the other women he'd dated, she had a mind

of her own, and aspirations. The best thing was that she wasn't afraid to keep him in check. It was obvious how much he'd changed since he'd gotten involved with her.

"I'm sorry for ruining your evening," I said, looking at her.

She smiled, rose from her chair, and took my hand. "Don't even apologize. This is more important than any dinner or movie."

"Thank you, but I still feel bad."

"Trust me. Marc cooked. I don't mind."

"Hey," Marc said, "I can cook."

"Anyway," Dahlia said with a roll of her eyes, "the movie wasn't important either."

"Well, I don't know about you, but I was looking forward to a little *Booty Call* tonight," Marc said with a laugh.

Doctor Chin laughed too.

"You'll be booty calling all by yourself if you don't shut up," Dahlia said, with a light tap to the back of his head.

I could only smile at their horseplay. I was glad that they were there.

I had just about calmed down, when a nurse ran into the waiting area. "Doctor Chin, we need you right away. Number two is having problems breathing again."

'Number two?' That was Isaiah's station. I grabbed the doctor's arm. "What's wrong with my son? Doctor, what's going on?"

He pulled away from me slowly. "Please stay here, Ms. Atkins. I'm going to go and have a look at him." He hurried down the hall with Marc, Dahlia and me right behind him.

I couldn't believe the commotion I saw all around Isaiah. I ran up to his bed and screamed his name. "Isaiah!"

His skin color was pasty white, and his breathing was even more constricted than when I'd first brought him in.

I reached out to touch him with trembling hands. "Help him, please! Do something! Isaiah!"

"Ms. Atkins," a nurse said, trying to push me away, "it's best right now if you go to the waiting area."

"I'm not leaving my son. Take your hands off of me!" I was insane with panic and fear.

The nurse did her best to move me back. "Ms. Atkins, Doctor Chin will do everything he can to help your son, I promise you. But right now, he needs to concentrate. And he can't do that with you here."

I looked over her shoulder and watched the doctor frantically work to get Isaiah's breathing back to normal. I shook my head. I didn't want to believe that he was in danger again.

"Please, Ms. Atkins," the nurse said, her voice soothing but firm.

I looked at her and shook my head no. I couldn't leave my son.

Marc appeared beside me. "Let's let them help Isaiah," he said softly. He gently put his arm around me and held me close to him.

I watched in dread as the doctor and his staff tried to get Isaiah's breathing under control. My head was ringing from the confusion, voices barking out different orders, machines beeping incessantly, shoes shuffling on the floor.

And then something dreadful happened.

"Flat line!"

I held my breath as Doctor Chin began to administer CPR. Over and over he pressed on my son's tiny chest. Over and over he gave him mouth to mouth.

Marc's grip around me tightened, Dahlia sobbed beside me.

"Don't die," I whispered. "Please God, don't take my baby away."

I stood unmoving, with tears pouring from my eyes and my body shivering from anxiety, until Doctor Chin looked up at the clock on the wall and in an eerily solemn voice said, "Time of death . . . eight thirty-nine."

I fainted after that.

Jocelyn

Icouldn't speak after David made his announcement to me. It was like something had swallowed my tongue and taken away my voice. I just sat silently while he got himself ready to go. Even after he left I didn't move. He had left me to go to New York to take care of his son. A son that he had with Janelle. A son he had kept hidden from me.

It took a while for what had happened to register, and when it finally sank in, I did the first thing that came to my mind—I flung the plates of food and glasses of wine from the table.

I was filled with so many different emotions—anger, pain, sadness, and confusion. I needed someone to talk to. I needed my sister.

I went to the couch and picked up the phone. When Mari answered I said, "He has a . . . son."

"What did you just say?"

"A son. He has a fucking son with Janelle." Angry tears started to fall from my eyes. I held the phone as if I was holding David's neck. "Mari, I need you. Please."

I lost whatever strength I had and let the phone drop from my hands to my lap and broke down.

In between my sobs, I could hear my sister calling out to me, but I couldn't respond. I was paralyzed with disbelief.

Just before I slid from the couch to the floor, I heard Mari say, "I'm coming over."

That made the tears fall harder from my eyes.

Marisol

When I arrived at Jocelyn's, I told myself that I wouldn't
say, "I told you so." I knew that she felt bad enough as
it was without having me rub anything in her face. But that
was exactly what I was thinking. I knew that something was
going to happen between her and David. Their relationship
had been too clean, too perfect. And my ex had taught me
the hard way just how "perfect" a relationship could really
be. Nothing was ever easy. Especially love.

I hadn't seen my sister since we last argued about Eric. I
had received all of her phone calls, but I just refused to return them. She needed to learn a lesson, and the only way
that was going to happen was by me not being there for her
for a little while. Like I said, she had to learn that her actions
had repercussions. I was her sister, and would do anything
for her, but that didn't mean that she could continue to use
me.

The only reason I didn't ignore her call this time was because I had planned on telling her that.

David had a baby with Janelle.

Damn. What a lesson to learn.

I didn't know what to think or say about that. I struggled with two different feelings. Half of me thought this was what she deserved for the pain she had caused Eric, but then the other half thought about how much of a spineless piece of shit David was for doing this to my sister. No matter what Jocelyn may have done, that part of me would always win.

I rang the doorbell and then tried the doorknob. Just as I had figured, it was unlocked. I walked in and immediately sighed when I saw Jocelyn slumped in front of the sofa.

I called her name and knelt down beside her.

"Hermanita," I said, pushing her hair away from her face, "don't cry, baby. Everything's going to be okay."

She looked up at me, her eyes swollen and red from crying. Her cheeks were flush. "I should've known something was going to happen," she said, draping her arms around my neck. "I should've known he was going to hurt me again. You were right, Mari. You warned me. You told me to be careful."

"Shhh," I said, caressing the back of her head. "Don't cry. You couldn't have prevented any of this. You had no way of knowing."

"He'd been traveling a lot over the past couple of months, but I thought it was for his book. I was so naïve. I thought he loved me. Mari, you told me, but I didn't listen."

I patted her head and let her cry. I was glad she had said it and not me. "Shh," I whispered softly. "Everything will be fine. Did he give you an explanation?"

She pushed away from me suddenly and stood up. I knew that within the phases of pain, first came the tears and next came the anger. I could see her brow crinkling and her hands clenching at her sides.

"He didn't say shit! Not one fucking word. He just said he had to go. His son was in the hospital. Some fucking explanation, right? Goddamn him!"

I stood up and went beside her. I didn't know what to say. I was speechless. "Well, you're better than I would've been,"

I finally said. "He wouldn't have been able to get out the door if it had been me. How did all of this happen?"

"Janelle called."

" 'Janelle'?"

"Yes, and I answered the phone."

"And what happened?"

"Nothing. She asked for David, and when she said who she was I was so shocked that I just gave him the phone."

I took Jocelyn's hand and led her back to the couch. "I had a long day at work, sis. The last thing I want to do right now is stand."

We sat down, and I kept her hand in mine.

"So, what do you want to do?"

She looked at me and bit on her quivering bottom lip. "I don't know." She laid her head on my shoulder. "I just don't know."

We sat in silence then, with her crying and me glad to be off my feet.

About twenty minutes passed before we spoke again. During that time, Jocelyn cried and then cursed and became silent, and then cried and cursed some more. I didn't try to stop her. I waited until I knew she was finished and then went to the refrigerator and poured a glass of juice for both of us.

"Okay, so listen," I said, handing her the drink, "what's our first step?"

" 'Our'?"

"Yes, our. Did you think I was going to let you go through this alone?"

"Mari, just you being here is enough."

"Yeah, well this ride's not over yet. This is a real-life novella. And you know how I like my stories."

"I know that we haven't spoken in a while. And I know it was my fault. I'm sorry for ever yelling at you. You were only looking out for me like you've always done."

"Don't worry about it," I said with a smile. I was glad she apologized, because I was upset at her. "We're sisters. We're not supposed to take each other's advice all the time. Now, how do you want to handle this?"

"I don't know. I feel so fucking betrayed. I mean, how could he not tell me he had a son? How could he have kept this secret from me?"

I sipped on my juice and sat back down on the couch. My feet were killing me. I had promised myself to get out of retail, but I didn't know what else to do. I hadn't finished college, and even if I had, I had no idea what I wanted to do. I always envied Jocelyn for that. Since junior high, she'd always known what she wanted out of life. But not me.

"Okay, listen," I said, taking a long gulp, "obviously, this happened before you two got together. To be brutally honest with you, this shouldn't have come as a big surprise. I don't like what he did just as much as you, but he was with Janelle, when you guys were sneaking around."

"Are you defending him?" she asked, turning around and glaring at me.

I quickly threw up my hands. "No, I'm not defending him. All I'm saying is that we need to hear his side to understand why he did what he did. It was 'chicken shit' of him. You and I both know that. But don't you want to know why? I think that we should at least hear what he has to say."

"I don't want to know. I'm through with him. He's hurt me for the last goddamned time."

"Look, Jocelyn, you may not want to know, but I do. *Hermanita,* I haven't had this much excitement since one of my former co-workers came in the store and accused me of sleeping with her husband, which I never did, by the way. He came on to me. Anyway, that was six, seven months ago. I need your drama to liven up my life."

"You're a trip."

"Yes, I am. And as your sister, I demand that you let him

explain first. I'll even give you a tape recorder. Just make sure you get all of the dirt, before you go off on him all you want."

"You're crazy," she said with a laugh.

I was glad to see her smiling. I couldn't take the tears too much longer. If there was one thing I got from my marriage, it was that I learned how to be a fighter. I couldn't stand women bitching and complaining. Men fed off of that shit. A crying woman always made their dicks and heads swell.

"All right look, right now the only thing you can do is relax. Let him handle his business. He's going to have to come home some time. And when he does, you can curse him out all you want. Just make sure you do it after you make his ass give you an explanation."

I swallowed the rest of my drink and patted the cushion next to me. "Now, let's kick back for some therapy. Pop in *Waiting to Exhale.*"

David

When I reached the Manhattan Bridge I tried Janelle's place one last time. I was praying that she would answer the phone because if she did then that meant everything was okay. When she didn't, I tried her and Marc's again. I got the same results.

I navigated my way through the city's traffic and hurried on to Beth Israel Hospital. I had a bad feeling brewing inside of me. My instincts were telling me that something wasn't right, and my instincts were usually never wrong.

After struggling to find a parking spot, I raced into the emergency room. As expected, it was crowded as shit, but I didn't care. I rushed up to the receptionist, a large black woman with straw for hair, and interrupted her as she was getting information from a thugged-out guy with a blood-stained bandage wrapped around his head.

"My son was brought here—Isaiah Joseph Atkins—I need to know where he is."

"Excuse me," the receptionist said, snapping her head back, "but don't you see me here with somebody?"

"Yeah, nigga," the thug wannabe said. "Bounce."

I turned to the guy. "Look, man, I just need to find out where my son is, so just hold tight." I turned back to the receptionist. "Isaiah Joseph Atkins."

"Yo, nigga. I don't give a shit about your son," the punk said, standing up in my face. I easily stood six inches taller than him and outweighed him by at least fifteen pounds.

"Listen, *nigga*, unless you want to need more bandages wrapped around your ass, I suggest you sit down, shut the fuck up and be patient." I leaned toward him so that he knew I was serious.

He looked at me for a few seconds, trying to decide if he could take me or not. Lucky for him he sat down.

I turned back to the receptionist and for the last time said, "Isaiah Joseph Atkins. Where is he?"

After getting the information I needed, I raced to where Isaiah was supposed to be. When I got there, the station was empty. Suddenly, someone called out my name from behind me. Marc.

I turned around and waited while he walked toward me slowly. It wasn't until he got close to me that I noticed his eyes were red and swollen. I didn't say a word, when he came up to me and put his hand on my shoulder.

He stared at me long and hard for a few seconds, and then a tear snaked from the corner of his eye.

"When?" I asked, my shoulders slumping.

"About two hours ago."

"How?"

"His attack was too severe for him. His body couldn't handle it. The doctors tried everything they could."

I took a deep breath and bit down on my lip. "I tried calling, but I couldn't get anyone."

"In the rush and panic we forgot our phones."

"Where's Janelle?"

"She took it pretty hard and passed out. The doctors revived her and then gave her something to calm her down. She was pretty hysterical. I'm sorry, man."

I didn't answer him. I just stood quiet and rested my hands on my hips. I didn't want to believe what he had told me. My son couldn't be dead.

I shook my head and bit back my tears. "Are the doctors in there with her now?"

"No. Just Dahlia."

"This can't be real, man. Tell me it's a nightmare I'm having and that I'm gonna wake up and everything will be back to normal."

"I wish I could. Believe me, I do."

I stepped away from him and leaned against the wall for support. My knees were wobbly and I felt like I was going to fall.

"Dead," I whispered. And then, without warning, my tears fell. I buried my hands in my face and refused to fight them.

Finally, I looked up at Marc, who had shed a few more of his own. "Take me to Janelle."

"Janelle," I whispered, stepping into the room. She was lying on her side in a fetal position, not moving.

Dahlia was sitting beside her. Her makeup had run from crying. With a nod, she moved away from the bed for me to take her place.

I sat down softly beside Janelle and gently touched her forehead.

She shuddered when I did.

I caressed her cheek, then her hand. "Everything's going to be okay," I whispered. "We'll get through this." A new wave of tears fell from my eyes and slid down my cheeks to my chin.

As they fell onto the bed, Janelle turned over and burrowed her body into mine. "I'm sorry," she said, "I'm so sorry I let this happen."

I wrapped my arms around her body and squeezed her tightly. "Shhh. This wasn't your fault. You couldn't have prevented this from happening."

"I was his mother. I should've known he had asthma. I should've known." Her body shook inside of my arms.

I kissed her forehead. "You couldn't have known. This wasn't your fault." I lay my head against her shoulder and rocked her slowly.

We cried and held onto one another until a nurse came and said that she needed the room.

I had only ever been to two funerals in my lifetime. One was for a friend of a friend, the other was for a former co-worker that I didn't know too well. Needless to say, Isaiah's funeral was a whole new and devastating experience for me. My family was there. I'd told them the news the day after Isaiah died. My mother couldn't stop crying; Isaiah had been her only grandchild. My father kept an expressionless mask on, which I expected. He rarely showed his true emotions, but I knew he was hurting. Because they lived in New York, they had been seeing Isaiah frequently.

Of course, I had been chewed out for not telling them when she was pregnant, but I didn't know how to. They still didn't know that I was back with Jocelyn. I'd just told them I had to get away from the city for a while.

My mom would have had a fit if she knew. She never did care too much for Jocelyn, although she never really said why. My father didn't really care one way or the other. I think his main concern was that I wasn't gay.

As far as they both knew, Janelle and I just couldn't get along and ended the relationship. Thankfully, they didn't know that I wasn't there when he was born, because Janelle had lied and told them that I had helped her deliver. That was typical, Janelle, always looking out for me. I owed her for that. Seemed like I owed her for a lot.

Tina, her husband, and Janelle's family all flew in from California. Janelle's mother was no worse off than my mother was. Janelle was her only child, and the loss of Isaiah was too much for her. She had to be removed and consoled as she cried hysterically. Janelle's father was a bit more expressive than my father and cried quietly.

Tina was broken up too, but checked her emotions enough so that she could be the shoulder Janelle desperately needed.

Besides our families, a few mutual friends attended and brought flowers and their sympathy. Other than Marc and a few co-workers, I hadn't told too many people, for fear of news getting back to Jocelyn.

The whole process had been hard. People shook my hand and said they were sorry and although their apologies were sincere, the only thing I wanted was for them to leave. I wanted to be alone with my son. I didn't want to share him or his soul with anyone.

I had a feeling Janelle wanted the same thing. Throughout the service, she sat unmoved, a veil covering her face. She didn't say a single word to anyone. It hurt to see her that way. I would have given anything to change what had happened.

As if the pain from Isaiah's death wasn't enough, I still hadn't gone home to Jocelyn. I wanted to, but I wasn't ready for the confrontation. I needed to postpone it for as long as I could. I had tried calling her once, though, to make an attempt to explain as best as I could, but as soon as she answered the phone, I knew there was no chance for that.

"What do you want, David?"

"I just want to talk for a little while. I want to explain a few things to you."

"Oh, so now you want to explain things? What happened during the nine months Janelle was pregnant? Didn't you think you had to explain anything then?"

I sighed. I didn't want to argue. "My son died, Jocelyn."

A few seconds of silence followed.

"I'm very sorry," she finally said, anger in her tone.

"Look, I know you're angry, but please give me a few days to sort things out here, then I'll come home and explain everything to you."

"David," she said, her tone subdued but still sharp, "I'm sorry about your loss, but what you did was still bullshit."

"Let's not do this now, Jocelyn."

"What? So I should wait again? How long this time?"

"Jocelyn, I said just give me a few days."

"I can't believe you did this to me."

"Jocelyn, keeping the truth from you wasn't an easy thing for me to do."

"So you think it's easier to explain after the fact?"

"I know it was wrong, and I'm sorry." I sighed. I really didn't need the argument.

"Spare me the fucking apologies. I thought our relationship meant something to you. Obviously, I was wrong."

"Jocelyn, please . . ."

"You know what, David—you go ahead and take your few days. But let me tell you, you're going to have to wait to talk until *I'm* ready. You do have time for that, don't you?"

"Jocelyn—"

Click.

Damn. I couldn't blame her for her anger, and I knew that I was pushing my luck more than I already had. I had to admit, though, I was glad to have everything out in the open. I just wished it didn't take losing my son for that to happen.

David

"I'm going home to face the music."

Marc looked at me with a raised eyebrow. "You ready?"

"No, but I have no choice. I can't put it off any longer. It's been a month. If it weren't for Janelle's condition, which still worries me, I would have gone home sooner."

"I wouldn't want to be in your shoes, bruh. I like them, they're cool and expensive, but I still wouldn't want to be in them."

"If I could get another pair, man, I would."

"How's Janelle anyway? I've been busy this past month with the opening of the new gym. I haven't been able to stop by or call like I wanted to. Plus, I'll admit, I've been reluctant to."

"That's understandable. *Surviving* is the best word I can use, man. That's about all she's doing. She's lost weight from not eating, and she hasn't started working yet. I've tried to get her to do both. I figured that some work, even if she does it from home, would help get her mind off of things. At least keep it occupied for a while. But she won't work, and I can't spoonfeed her, you know what I mean?"

"Yeah. She just needs more time. Isaiah was everything to her."

"I know. He was to me too."

We sat silently for a few minutes after that and stared at the television screen above the bar. I knew what he meant about Isaiah being everything to Janelle. He and Janelle had become good friends, and even though he was still my boy, he didn't like what I had done, or at least how I did it. I couldn't blame him. I felt more and more regretful for the pain that I had caused her.

"I miss him, man. It's hard to believe he's gone. Sometimes I feel like if I would've been here, none of this would have happened. Like this is God's way of punishing me for what I did."

"You and I both know there was no way to prevent what happened. The doctor already confirmed that. And God can be tough sometimes, but if he did this to punish you, then he's pretty damn cruel. And we both know he's not that."

"So, why'd it happen?" I lowered my head and closed my eyes tightly to keep myself from crying. "Why did he have to die?" I asked quietly. I looked up at him, hoping he had the answer.

He continued to stare deadpan at the TV and took a sip of his beer. "I don't know, man," he said softly. "I guess his purpose was served, and it was just his time."

Neither one of us spoke after that. We watched the basketball game and downed the rest of our beers in silence.

Jocelyn

It took every bit of my strength not to swing at David, when he walked through the front door. I wanted to go ballistic but, instead, decided to take Marisol's advice and listen to what he had to say. I bit down on my tongue, turned my back on him, walked into the living room to sit down, and waited. And breathed. Oh, did I breathe. One through ten—over and over again. It didn't help, though, so I squeezed the hell out of the cushion and waited for him to make the first move.

I stayed silent when he sat down beside me. At least he was smart enough to not reach out toward me.

Instead, he sat there, cracked his knuckles a few times, and cleared his throat.

I could tell he was nervous. *Good.*

We sat there for a few minutes, saying nothing. I was getting angrier by the second.

Finally, he worked up the nerve to open his mouth. "I missed you."

That did it. I couldn't hold back any longer. "You have a lot of fucking balls—I'll give you that."

"Jocelyn, I didn't know how to tell you."

"You had a son. I don't see how you couldn't have told me that!"

"What? And risk losing you?"

"Who the hell said you would've lost me?"

"Come on. You and I both know how upset you would've been."

"Upset, yeah. But shit happens, David. You and Janelle were engaged. You two had sex. Things happen. But to not tell me?" I slammed my hand on the cushion. "I think I deserve more credit than that."

"I'm sorry," David said, his voice sounding absolutely pathetic to me.

"Are you?" I stood up and walked away from him. My hands were getting sweaty and I could feel my temperature rising.

I turned and faced him. He looked terrible. His eyes were sunken and dark. He had a slight beard and I knew how much he hated facial hair. He had also lost a lot of weight. I wanted to feel bad for him. I really did, but I just couldn't.

"Are you really sorry?"

"What do you mean by that? Do you think it was easy for me to hide Isaiah's existence from you?"

"You tell me," I said, staring at him coldly.

"Damn it! I battled with it every day. I didn't want to lose you. I just didn't know how to tell you. Eventually, more and more time passed, and it just became impossible."

" 'Impossible'? So when were you going to tell me?—At his fucking graduation?"

"Jocelyn." He stood up and reached out for me.

I quickly stepped away and raised my hands. "Don't even think about touching me!" I said vehemently.

"Jocelyn . . ."

"So what other lies have you told me? Are there any other kids? Any other women?" I tapped my right foot on the ground a couple of times and placed my hands on my hips.

"No! There's nothing else."

"You lied to me time and time again, David. Just once, did you ever think about being a fucking man?"

"Jocelyn . . ."

"Were you still fucking Janelle? Did you ever really let that relationship go?"

"Come on!"

"Come on, what? You spent weekends in New York. I know you didn't spend the time with him alone. It's not so far-fetched that you couldn't have fallen back in love with her. Shit, maybe you never fell out of love."

I walked away from him, into the kitchen. I needed as much distance between us as possible. We had lied to be to-gether. He'd told Janelle that he was going away for the weekend on *business*. I can't believe I was stupid enough to fall for the same lines.

David approached me, but knew where to stop. He hung his head low and laid his hands behind his neck. "When Janelle told me she was pregnant, I didn't know what to think. I was shocked. We argued about it. I even asked her whose it could've been, even though I knew.

"You and I had both sacrificed so much to be together, I was afraid to tell you. I tried to avoid the situation altogether and focus on us. Shit, Isaiah was two months before I even saw him. But when I did, I knew that I had to be a father to him. I also knew that too much time had passed and telling you wasn't an option. At least not until I thought of a way to do it. But that way never came up. Believe me, the last thing I wanted was for you to find out the way you did."

"You didn't see your son for two months? What the hell kind of man are you? How could I have ever thought that I'd be happy with you?"

"Jocelyn, please . . . this wasn't easy."

I took a deep breath and thought back to that night. I

thought about the shock that I felt when he said the word *son*. His *son*. It was like a hard, quick slap. I didn't have time to react to it. And when I finally did, he was gone. That hurt me the most.

"David, I'm sorry that your son died. I'm sorry that you've had to go through this pain. But you betrayed me—better yet, you betrayed us. We were supposed to be a team."

"We *are* a team."

"Not when you do things like that, we aren't. After everything we've been through together, past and present, how could you have done this to me?"

"I'm sorry."

"Sorry isn't good enough."

"Please, Jocelyn. I need you."

"You didn't need me when you couldn't tell me the truth," I snapped.

"Give me a chance to make it up to you," he pleaded.

"It took years apart for that to happen before. Instead of going forward, you went backward. How am I supposed to have confidence in you now?" I could feel tears snaking away from the corners of my eyes. I didn't want to cry in front of him, but I felt so used. I leaned against the kitchen counter and wrapped myself in my arms. The tears wouldn't stop coming.

"What do I have to do, Jocelyn?"

"Give me time."

"Time for what?"

"I don't know. Just give me some fucking time! Time to figure out what I want and need."

"'Want and need'? How could you not know? Damn, Jocelyn, my son just died. Can't you at least be a little more sympathetic to how *I'm* feeling right now?"

"You want sympathy? Why? You didn't need me before." I didn't want to argue anymore. I didn't even want to speak. All of the fight had gone out of me.

"Shit, how many times do I have to tell you that it wasn't that easy to tell you?" David yelled out.

"You never fucking tried!"

He didn't say a word after that. I was right, and he knew it. He never gave me the opportunity to bitch and complain, or maybe even understand his dilemma.

"Jocelyn."

"Can you leave, please? I need to be alone right now. I need to think."

"This is my home too."

"Fine! I'll leave."

I moved away from the counter and walked past him without a word. I went upstairs, packed a few things and then came back downstairs. He was standing in the living room, stoic and silent. I opened my mouth to say something but then changed my mind. There was nothing else for me to say. I walked out the door and slammed it shut behind me. The bastard never even tried to stop me.

Marc

"Why is my life falling completely apart? Shit, I'm not a terrible guy. There are other people in this world that have done worse things, you know what I mean?"

"I feel for you, man."

"So, why the fuck am I being punished like this? Shit!"

I could only stay silent and let him vent his frustrations. Besides, it wouldn't have been good for me to give him my opinion. But, let's face it, none of this would have happened if he didn't send that e-mail. But I wasn't about to tell him that. I did feel bad for him, though, because he was right—he wasn't a bad guy at all.

If it ever came down to it, I'd never hesitate to put my life in his hands. With the exception of what went down with Janelle, Dave was one of the most stand-up, selfless guys I knew. I could definitely understand his argument because murderers went through less shit than he was going through. I felt for him. He lost Janelle. He lost his son. Now, he was on the verge of losing Jocelyn—again.

"Don't I deserve to win something?" he continued. "Shit, I'm losing it all."

"I feel for you, but you have to relax."

" 'Relax'? I went from having it all to having nothing."

"Maybe you won't lose Jocelyn," I added quickly.

"Marc, I know Jocelyn. She's not coming back."

"Give her time."

"I'm sick of time."

I listened to him sigh heavily into the phone and shook my head. I was glad we weren't in the same room. I knew how he got when shit went into the dumpster for him. He could wrestle the hell out of an alligator if he had to, but when it came to dealing with his own life, man, could he whine. He had absolutely no patience.

"Look, Dave, you're gonna have to give Jocelyn some time to sort things out. The reality is, you should've told her a lot sooner, and you know that."

"Yeah, I know, but . . ."

"No buts, man. That's just how it is. Plus she's a woman and she's got her blinders on right now. She's not about to see things your way."

"Man, why did all of this have to happen? I dream about Isaiah almost every night. I dream that I'm holding him, and then teaching him how to ride a bike, and then teaching him about girls. I've never felt pain like this before. Never! I feel so empty right now."

"I understand," I said softly. And I really did.

I had looked forward to being Uncle Marc. I couldn't wait to bring him presents and watch him grow up. I was looking forward to seeing him play with the kids that I planned on having, which was a real possibility, because I was going to propose to Dahlia.

I still remember when the doctor pronounced Isaiah's death. I held onto Janelle tightly when she fainted, but I'd come damn close to passing out myself. That was the hardest thing I ever had to go through.

Having to watch Dave suffer wasn't easy either. When he

wasn't at Janelle's trying to help her, he would sit around my place and mope. He didn't eat. He barely slept. I even tried to get him to come to the gym with me, but he refused.

Within weeks, he went from being a pretty boy to looking like a black version of Tom Hanks in the movie *Cast Away*. Well, maybe not that drastic, but pretty damn close. I didn't know how to help him, so when he told me he was going home, I was happy. Not only because he was going to face his problems head on, but because it also meant that I wouldn't have to see his depression on a day-to-day basis. He was my brother for life, but it was tough seeing him like that.

"I miss Isaiah too, man."

"Man, Jocelyn didn't even care about my feelings. It was all about her. I couldn't even get a fucking hug. I know I was wrong, but damn, all I wanted from her was a little compassion."

"Just give her time. That's all you can do. Hopefully she'll come around. Then maybe you guys can work everything out. Time, my brother."

"And in the meantime, what the hell am I supposed to do?"

"Survive, bro. Write your book, pay your bills, work out. Survive. Because you can be sure she's going to do that too."

"Yeah."

When I hung up the phone, Dahlia had just walked in the door. We'd both decided to take the big step and move in together. We wanted to know if we could stand each other and our bad habits.

She moved into my place because it was bigger. Of course, it no longer looked like my place. It didn't take long for her to put a woman's touch on everything. The bathroom soap included.

"Hey, queen," I said, walking toward her. No matter what she wore or how little make-up she had on, I always got a rise out of her. I kissed her on the lips and squeezed her rear end.

She smiled and lightly brushed my manhood. "Hey, you. How was your day?"

"Not bad. I just got off the phone with Dave right before you walked in."

"How is he?"

"Jocelyn left."

"I expected that."

"Yeah, me too."

"How's he handling it?"

"You know Dave."

"Not well, huh?"

"No, not at all, but he'll get past it eventually. But anyway . . ." I took her into my arms, stared into her oval brown eyes and kissed her forehead.

Her forehead was one of my favorite features. It wasn't small, yet not too big, although she would disagree. When she pulled her hair back into a ponytail, like she had then, it gave her a totally different look. She reminded me of Pocahontas with curly hair.

I kissed her forehead again, then her soft lips, and at that moment, it became the right time. "Stay right here."

"What? Why?"

"You'll see. Just don't move." I quickly left the room and ran into the bedroom. When I came back she had her eyes squinted and her arms crossed.

"What are you up to?"

I wrapped my arms around her again and gave a light kiss to her cheek. "Dave's not the only one with problems. We've got some of our own."

"What do you mean, problems?" She knew I was up to something.

"I found something, and I don't know who it belongs to."

"What?"

I slid my hand into my pocket and removed the ring box with the engagement ring inside. Before I even handed it to her, tears began to well in her eyes.

"I found this box, and I don't know who it belongs to. The bad thing is, I can't get the damn thing open to see what's inside. Can you help me?" I took her hand, which was trembling slightly, and placed it in her palm.

She looked at me and then looked at the box.

"I must have worked out too hard or something," I said, smiling at her silence. "Give it a try."

"Oh . . ." she whispered. When she opened it, the tears fell down across her cheeks.

I took the two-karat Marquise diamond ring and slid it onto her finger. "Will you marry me?"

Her kiss answered my question.

Jocelyn

I didn't want to go to Mari's place, because I didn't want to have to talk about anything, so I rented a room at a hotel and stayed there for a few days. I just needed to be alone to think. My heart was broken and bleeding; David hurt me more than he could ever have realized. His lies took me right back to the past, when he'd cheated on me. The pain I felt then was almost unbearable. He was my first love and after I had invested so much time and energy in him, he turned right around and put that energy into someone else—literally. I wanted to kill him that night, but it hurt so badly that all I ended up doing was crying. It seemed like I cried for days. I ignored his phone calls. I ignored his knocks on my window. I didn't want to have anything to do with him. It took me a long time to get past the pain, after we broke up.

He may not have cheated on me with Janelle, at least he claimed he hadn't, but it felt like he did. I gave up my marriage for what I believed was going to be a faithful and undying love with him. I had never imagined that he would have hurt me again. Not that way.

Finding out he had a child on the way *would* have stung in the beginning, but I could have dealt with it. But instead of trusting in us, he lied. I would never have lied to him. Never. And as naïve as it may seem, I had never expected him to lie to me.

Marisol had been so right. She'd told me not to jump into anything too quickly, to really consider what I was doing. Unfortunately, I didn't listen to her. I thought I knew what I was doing. Obviously, leaving Eric to go back to David was a mistake.

Speaking of Eric, I missed his stability. He'd worked so hard to provide the life that we both had wanted. A life that maybe I wanted more than he did. I could always count on him to be there for me, and I knew that he would never have lied. Why did I have to hurt him the way I did? Why had I been so selfish?

Damn it, David.

More than nine months had passed without him telling me. What the hell kind of love was that? The more I thought about it, the more it hurt. I needed to occupy my mind with something, anything else. I needed to talk to someone. Someone who wouldn't tell me what I should or shouldn't have done. Someone who would just talk to me. I knew who that someone was. I just didn't know how he was going to respond.

Eric

"Hello, Eric."

More than a year had passed since I last spoke with Jocelyn. We didn't even speak when the divorce was made final. So when she called me, her voice was the last one I expected to hear coming from the other end of the line. I was happy to hear her voice though.

Since she'd left me, I'd kept pretty much to myself. Actually, I did what came naturally and buried myself in my work. I took on case after case, not because they interested me or because I thought I could win them, but because they kept me occupied. I figured the more work I did, the less time I had to dwell on the failure of my marriage, which also meant there was less time for me to blame myself for what had gone wrong.

The first couple of months were extremely hard for me. I wasn't used to being without her. My mornings were empty. My afternoons weren't the same, because I had no one to call and say hello. Even when I worked seventy to eighty hours a week, I was still comforted because I knew that I would be lying next to her at night. After she left, it took me a while to get used to an empty bed. I guess I never realized how big a role she had been playing in my everyday life.

The strain of being alone eased over time, but it was still hard on me, especially at business functions, where I would show up alone and everyone else had their husband or wife at their side. After the divorce, I felt like the talk of the town. I would catch a whisper here or a whisper there. Even when people weren't talking, their stares said it all. But I learned to cope.

The one thing I hadn't done since the divorce was date. Dating was never my strong area. I'd gone out on a few dates that friends had fixed up for me, but I could never find the connection that I longed for—the connection I had felt when Jocelyn and I were together. So to keep me company, I bought a cat. A gray Burmese I named Grady. I bought him more for the company than the affection. With Grady, I'd learned to deal with life without Jocelyn. So her call was like a monkey wrench being thrown into a puzzle that I had finally managed to rebuild. I should have been resentful. After all, she did leave me for another man. But I wasn't bothered at all.

"Hello, Jocelyn," I said, hiding my surprise.

"How have you been?"

I could hear a strain in her voice that I recognized and didn't like. "I'm fine. How are you?" I asked, not letting on that I noticed the tension.

"I'm . . . fine."

"I'll be honest, I'm a little surprised to be hearing your voice. You're not calling to ask for another divorce, are you? Because you can only do that once." I didn't really mean that last comment, but I didn't want to make the call too easy.

"No, Eric." She sighed into the receiver. "I'm just calling to say hello. I was thinking . . . you just came into my mind, that's all."

"Oh, I see. Well, it's nice to be thought of from time to time. So, how are things going for you—your job, I mean."

"The job is the same. Nothing new. What about you? Last time we spoke you had just been made a partner."

"I'm up to my neck in work, but that's the profession I chose, I guess. Some of the people in the beginning had a hard time dealing with a black partner, but my win percentage quickly helped them to see past that."

"That's good. I'm . . . happy for you."

I heard her start sniffling. I could tell that she had moved away from the phone. Pressing my ear harder into the receiver, I could hear her crying softly.

When she got back on, she cleared her throat. "I'm sorry," she said. "I got something caught in my throat."

Grady walked toward me and rubbed himself against my leg. I picked him up and rubbed the top of his head.

"Do you want to meet somewhere and talk?" I said, staring at Grady, who stared back at me and blinked.

It took Jocelyn a few seconds to answer. When she did, I could tell that she was going to crack. I didn't want to be on the phone when she did.

"How does an hour at Cheesecake Factory by the harbor sound? I'll go ahead and put our name on the list."

"Sounds good," she answered quietly.

"I'll see you then." I hung up the phone quickly, before anything else could be said.

She was in pain, and that bothered me. I never liked seeing or hearing her cry. It seemed like it took me forever to get to a point where I felt I was getting over her, but damn if she wasn't pulling me back in again . . .

*   *   *

It was like déjà vu all over again as Jocelyn and I sat across from one another. We were tucked away in a booth toward the back, and oddly enough, the restaurant was not crowded at all. It was perfect if you wanted a nice romantic evening, but a little awkward for two ex-lovers. We sipped water from our glasses and made small talk mostly about work.

As we spoke back and forth, I studied her. She looked almost the same. Her hair was still long and curly. Her figure was still shapely, despite the fact that it looked like she had lost a little weight. I tried not to speculate why. Her eyes were still mesmerizing, though red and slightly swollen from crying.

I took a quick moment to glance at her hand. I admit, my heart did a double-step, when I didn't see a ring on her finger. I wished she didn't have so much of an effect on me.

After the waiter took our orders, I decided to brave the waters a little bit. Besides, we couldn't talk about work all evening long.

"So," I said, watching her closely, "how have you been . . . really?"

She held both hands around her glass and lowered her head. She was holding back tears, I could tell.

Finally, she looked up at me. "How bad did I hurt you, Eric?"

The question threw me for a loop, and for a minute, I didn't know how to answer.

"You broke my heart, Jocelyn," I said as honestly as I could.

"I never meant to."

"People don't mean to do a lot of things."

"I'm sorry."

I took a sip of soda and nodded my head. "It's the past now."

"You never made me unhappy, at least not like I made you feel you did."

"I tried my best. Obviously, it wasn't enough." I was gripping my glass tightly as I spoke. I was filled with a combination of anger and pain that I had never actually expressed to her before.

To be honest, I'd never really vented in any way. I just kept my emotions bottled up inside until I thought the feelings went away.

"It wasn't you. It was me."

"Why are you telling me this? What do you want?"

"I just want to talk."

"Talk about what? *You* made the decision to leave *me,* remember? Not me."

"I know. Believe me, I know."

I watched her as she turned her head away from me and took a deep breath. She was hurting so badly, and I was trying not to let her know that it bothered me. Still, it wasn't easy for me to sit there and not reach out to her.

Damn her for making me care for her so much. I gave in. I picked up my napkin, reached across the table, and wiped away the tears that were falling.

Before I could pull away, she took hold of my hand and held it against her cheek.

I exhaled from the heat of her skin.

"I've missed you," she said as tears fell and wet my hand. "I've missed us."

I sat silently as she kept a firm but gentle hold on my hand. I didn't know what to say or think. Obviously something happened with her new relationship, but I didn't want to know what. I'd made up my mind that I wasn't going to ask. "I'm still the same person as before."

"I know, and I've missed that person."

"What do you want?" I asked again, although my voice had a slight tremble to it. "What are you trying to tell me?"

Just then, the waiter arrived with our food. Realizing what was going on, he did a nice thing and pretended like the food wasn't ours and quickly walked away. I made a note to leave a generous tip.

"What do you want?" I pressed again, as we were once again alone.

She let go of my hand and wiped her eyes with the napkin, and then she looked up at me.

If she only knew how badly I wanted to take her in my arms. Instead, I sat unflinching and speechless.

"Can we take a walk?" she said softly.

I watched her and then nodded.

The night was actually perfect for it. When we rose from the booth, I pulled out a fifty-dollar bill and left it by my glass of soda. Without thinking, I took Jocelyn's hand and headed toward the exit.

As we were leaving, we passed our waiter, who made subtle eye contact with me. I gave him a nod and motioned toward the booth. I knew that he had gotten his tip before we stepped out of the restaurant.

Janelle

Other than David, I hadn't told anyone that I was going to move back home. When Isaiah died, a part of me did too. Life for me in New York no longer had any meaning. I just seemed to be existing. Functioning had become a day-to-day struggle. I didn't have to worry about work because my boss called and said that I could take as much time off as I needed. I appreciated that. The only problem was that I had no desire to return to work. Being an editor was almost like being a writer. My ideas and thoughts also went into the creation of the story. But with my passion gone, I knew that I couldn't work the way I used to. I needed a fresh start of some kind. I needed fresh surroundings. Just being in the condo alone was almost enough to drive me insane.

Three months had passed, but I still woke up frequently at night to the imaginary sounds of Isaiah's cries. When I wasn't waking up, I was having nightmares about bringing Isaiah home in a casket.

My family and friends had tried to help me as best as they could. Tina stayed with me again, and so did my parents. They forced me to eat when I didn't want to and helped me sleep when I couldn't. Best of all, they let me cry when I couldn't hold the tears back. Even David, who had stayed with Marc, had been there for me. Despite his pain, he took care of all of the funeral preparations. He came over and checked on me frequently, oftentimes cooking or bringing takeout. He took me out for walks just to get me away from the apartment and bad memories. We even went to movies and shows.

David did his best to cheer me up, but it was obvious how much he had been affected. He had lost weight. He had dark circles under his eyes and a slight beard, because he wasn't shaving.

It hurt to see him so broken. I'd always hated seeing him in any kind of pain. There were times when I just wanted to wrap my arms around his neck, pull him toward me, and let him cry on my shoulders. I would've let my tears fall too. I missed us being able to lean on each other that way. I missed having his arm wrapped around me at night while he slept behind me.

When he betrayed me, I felt like all of the comfort I'd had was snatched away. Nothing felt safe anymore. It seemed like everyone had an agenda of some kind. I couldn't trust smiles or nods hello. The comfort didn't come back until Isaiah was born. I couldn't bring myself to trust anyone, but I trusted Isaiah. I knew that for as long as he lived, he was never going to hurt me. Now he was gone and I was alone again. That's why staying in New York was no longer an option.

I didn't have to call my parents to ask them if I could go back home. All I had to do was buy a ticket and show up at their front door. That's what I planned to do.

Telling David had been harder for me than I thought it was going to be. Despite everything we had been through, telling him was like hammering the final nail in a coffin of hope that I'd had open since he started being a father.

"When?" he asked.

"I'm not sure. I just made my decision. I've got a lot of things to do before I can leave."

"Are you sure you've thought about it?"

"Yes, I have. I can't stay in New York anymore. There's nothing here for me. Just pain. Too much pain. I just need to get away from here. I need new scenery."

"Okay."

His reaction got to me a little. I guess I was hoping for a little more resistance from him. If he'd asked me to stay I might have given my decision a second thought. But his nonchalance just showed me that it was better for me to just make a clean getaway and leave my old life.

David

"I can't believe you're getting married, man." I looked at my boy and smiled.

"Bruh, she's the one," Marc said with a smile.

"I'm happy for you." This had been my first time back to New York since Jocelyn left more than two months ago. I hadn't seen Marc since then, so this was our night out to celebrate his engagement.

During the time Jocelyn was gone, I didn't do anything but write. I wrote day and night, nonstop. I actually threw away the novel I had been working on previously and started a brand new one. This one was completely different from my others. I was actually writing a love story.

Marc was right. Writing was what I needed to get back into. It helped me to survive being alone. I think I really needed that time, anyway, to figure out what was important to me. I realized a lot of things I'd done wrong, especially when it came to Janelle.

I'd called her a few times to make sure that she was all right. We'd spoken a lot, actually. It got to me when she told me of her plans to move back to California, but I didn't show it. I understood her reasons for wanting to leave, but a big part of me didn't want her to go. In my solitude, I'd come to realize just how much she meant to me.

Jocelyn and I had a special love, but with Janelle, I knew hers was unconditional. The only reason I didn't try to change her mind about leaving was because I didn't feel that I had a right to. If I had never sent that e-mail, none of this would have ever happened. How could I ask her to stay knowing that?

I hadn't heard from Jocelyn since she left, but I knew that she had come by, because I came home one day and saw that some of her things were gone. But that was fine with me because being alone gave me time to think about what was and wasn't important. I realized that the past should stay right where it was . . . in the past.

Jocelyn's reaction to Isaiah's death also helped me see that what we had wasn't as real as I'd thought it was. She never seemed to care about my feelings when I told her. She was so concerned about herself. I knew I had done the wrong thing, but I was hurting so much inside, a little compassion would have meant so much to me. But she was incapable of doing that. She talked so much about me not treating our relationship as a team, but she was doing the same thing to me. That was the one major difference between her and Janelle. Janelle would have been mad, but she would never have let me hurt alone like that.

My love for Jocelyn would never change. I knew that. She was, after all, my first love. I would always hold a special place in my heart for her. But after the dust had settled and I started to see clearly, I realized where I belonged.

"I don't want Janelle to leave," I declared.

"Then don't let her, bruh," Marc said, his eyes glued to the game above the bar. "Be a man and don't let her go."

"What if I can't get her to stay?"

"Then at least you tried and failed like a man."

"She really is special."

"I told you that a long time ago, but your head was all screwed up. You were looking behind you instead of in front of you. You weren't trying to hear anything."

"A light tap wouldn't have been bad."

"Yeah, but then we would've fought. and I would've won. And you know what happens after that. Your mom would've cursed my ass out."

"Yeah, whatever, man."

We laughed and then turned away from the game. It was halftime.

"Damn, I can't believe I fucked things up the way I did."

"You're a man. It's in our nature. But we learn. It may take us fifty tries, but eventually we learn."

"She's getting set to leave next weekend."

"So, why are you still watching the game with me?"

Without another word, I slid off my stool and gave him a pound.

"One question before you go."

"What's that?"

Marc stared at me seriously. "What if Jocelyn comes back?"

"She's not coming back."

"But what if she does and wants to work things out?"

I thought about his question for a moment and then smiled. No more words were needed. He nodded. I turned and left.

Later that night, as Sade sang to me in the background, I sat in front of my laptop and thought about Marc's question to me—what if Jocelyn came back?

Since our breakup, neither one of us had tried to contact the other. And until Marc's question to me, I was content with that. But his question made me realize that if I was determined to go forward, I needed to close the door behind me for good. And I knew of only one way to do that. So, I sent an e-mail.

After I hit send, I thought about Janelle. I was extremely nervous about what I was going to do. I didn't know how she was going to react. At first, I was going to head over to her place right after I left Marc at the bar, but then I changed my mind. I thought about all of the things that Janelle and I had gone through. I contemplated all that I had put her through and wondered if it was really worth it to try and win her back. I had no clue. But I knew I wanted to try.

Eric

Jocelyn was sleeping when I decided to leave her. I was staring out of the bedroom window, looking at the full moon in the night sky. From time to time, I would glance back at Jocelyn and then look back to the moon. We'd been together since leaving the restaurant months before. I can't say that I hadn't been happy, because I was. I loved Jocelyn more than I'd ever loved any other woman before, and having her back in my life made me almost whole again. Almost. But there was something missing. And it wasn't until I stared at that moon that I realized what it was.

There was once a time when, like the moon, her spirit and presence would have brought light to my darkest hours. But looking back at her, I realized that her beauty was no longer the same. It was tainted. I'd been feeling that way for a long time, but I tried not to admit it. I didn't want to believe that my feelings for her had changed. I didn't want to admit that I didn't love Jocelyn anymore, at least not the way I used to. And I don't think that she really loved me the same either. I think I was her fallback when things didn't go her way. I think she loved the idea of being with me and not being alone.

Knowing in my heart that I wasn't completely and uncond
ditionally loved left me with just one option—I had to leave.

Making sure not to wake her, I got up from the bed and got dressed and then wrote her a note saying one thing: Good-bye. I know it seemed like a cold thing to do, but after what she'd done to me, I think a little callousness on my part was due.

I laid the note on her dresser when I was finished and then kissed her gently one last time. Even with my good-bye, I knew that I would always love her. But her love had been given to someone else, and I couldn't get past that. I left knowing that I made the right decision.

Jocelyn

Jocelyn,

How are you doing? I hope things are going well for you. I know you are surprised to see this coming from me, and I know that you probably don't want to read this, but please, don't delete it before you read it the whole way through. I guess things didn't go the way we planned. And I know that I am to blame for that. I accept that. I'm sorry for the pain I caused you. I'm sorry for making you feel as though I didn't believe in our love enough to confide in you when I should have. But I really did believe in our love, and I really wanted to go the distance with you.

However, in our time apart, I've come to realize something important. Although we may have had a special kind of love, it was never meant to be for us. We were each other's first love and what we shared will never be forgotten. But our lives were predestined to go separate ways. And no matter how intensely we loved, there was no escaping our destiny. I'm glad to have met you, Jocelyn. I'm glad to have received your love. I will always cherish the memory of us. I will always cherish having been a part of each other's lives.

But now the time has come for us to take the paths that have always been there for us. Follow yours carefully. I hope that you find the true happiness that you deserve. Good-bye, Jocelyn.

David

I deleted David's message, shut off my laptop and turned off all the lights, leaving me alone in the dark. *Good-bye.* He'd said good-bye. It had been so painfully final, but in a lot of ways, it was necessary. I knew then that we weren't meant to be, but I think somewhere deep down inside of me I wished for another chance. David's e-mail was kind of like the final nail in the coffin to our past. It was the right thing to do.

Tears fell from the corner of my eyes, as I reflected on the life I'd had with Eric. So many women complained day after day about not having a good man. But I never could. Eric wasn't a freeloader. He was about something, and he was successful. He was faithful. He was respectful. He treated me like I was a queen. *I gave up the life I had with him for David?* I wiped a few tears away and thought that at that moment, *there was no bigger fool.*

I exhaled softly and wiped away more tears. David had followed his path, and Eric had chosen his. I was faced with the reality that I had to find my own.

Janelle

Packing and moving were never my favorite things to do. I hated the whole process of boxing and taping. I always avoided them when I could. As luck would have it, I had decided to move on a weekend when everyone was going to be out of town. Even David, who had offered to help me weeks before, called at the last minute to cancel because "something came up." I bet something did. More like someone. Jocelyn probably came back home. They probably decided to work out their problems.

I remember when he told me what had happened. The whole story really took me by surprise. I was in complete shock. I didn't know that he hadn't told her about Isaiah, so I couldn't blame her for being upset. I would've been too, but I don't know if I would have left him at that particular moment. I don't think I could've left him alone after knowing what happened. Shows the kind of love she had. Of course, I didn't say that to him. I just kept those thoughts to myself. David lied to me, then he lied to her. Served both of them right.

But I still felt bad for David. We'd made a lot of progress

since our split. We seemed to rediscover the special friend-ship that we had lost. I was really looking forward to seeing him. Getting close again gave me false hopes of us somehow being together again, but I guess the "something" that had come up was more important.

Since everyone bailed on me, I decided to call a moving company and save myself the headache.

David felt bad about not being there and insisted on call-ing a company for me. I thanked him and then said good-bye. That was the hard part: saying good-bye. How do you say good-bye to the one you love? I think that's a song.

I had to hold back tears when we spoke, because I didn't want him to know that I still loved him the way I did. I don't know if he would have realized that I was crying anyway, be-cause it seemed like he was in a hurry to get off the phone, so I didn't keep him.

Now that I'd taken care of everything else, I just had to wait. I sat down and exhaled. I was ready to start again.

When the bell rang, my heart jumped. I had dozed off, and of all people, I was dreaming about David. It was a hot dream too. I felt like telling whoever it was to leave and come back later so I could go back to sleep and finish get-ting my groove on. I hadn't had any in a long time. But who-ever was at the door was insistent because they rang the doorbell again. I got up reluctantly.

"I'm coming."

Before I stepped to the door, I took a moment to glance around the living room. Memories, both good and bad, seemed to float in the air around me. I was looking forward to leaving them all behind.

The bell rang again for the third time. *What part of "I'm coming" did they not understand?* I looked through the peep-hole but couldn't see anything because the hole was covered.

"Who's there?" I asked hesitantly.

"Second Chance Moving Company," a muffled Jamaican voice answered.

" 'Second Chance'?"

"Yes. A David Cray call us and tell us to be 'ere."

"Oh, okay. Sorry to keep you standing out there." I opened the door to the sight of David holding a bouquet of red roses. My heart skipped a beat.

"These are for you," he said, handing me the roses.

"What are you doing here? I thought you had something to do."

"This is what I had to do."

I was feeling warm all over, and my knees felt weak. I inhaled the roses' fragrance. "I don't understand."

David approached me and took one of my hands in his. "Janelle, I debated about how I would say what I have to say to you. I didn't know if you would scream at me, try to kick me, throw something at me, or maybe even worse, so I'll just be straightforward with you. Let me take a deep breath first."

He did, and so did I.

My heart was beating as if it were a drum in a salsa band.

"Janelle," he continued after what seemed like a day long pause, "I'm sorry for everything I've put you through, and I am truly sorry for all of the pain I've caused you. I know what I did was terrible and almost unforgivable. But what I'm asking you to do is to forgive me, because I've come to realize something very important these last couple of months. I've come to know that, without a doubt, I don't want to be without you. I love you. I love you more than I even knew. You are my best friend, and *you* are my true love. I've never been more sure of anything in my life. I don't want you to leave. Now. Or ever. Baby, please give me a second chance to show you how serious I am about you and about us."

I was speechless for a long while, as he watched me. I couldn't believe that he'd stood in front of me and poured his heart out the way he did. Although he didn't know it, he'd said so many things that I wanted to hear. But I'd been a fool once.

"David, I can't."

"Janelle, please, give me—give us another chance?"

"How do I know you won't hurt me again?"

"Because I won't."

"After all you've done, how do you expect me to trust you? I mean, come on, David. I'm not a fool. I know you're only here because Jocelyn left you."

"That's not true, Janelle. My being here has nothing to do with Jocelyn and I being over. I love you. Shit, I love you so much it hurts. But it hurts even more not being with you. I miss your company. I miss your touch. I miss you. Please give us another chance?"

As he waited for my answer, tears welled in my eyes. Every fiber of my being wanted to drop the flowers, wrap my arms around his neck, kiss him, and do what he was asking me to do and give us another chance. I've never loved any man like I loved David. But no man had ever hurt me the way he did. As tears ran down my cheeks I shook my head slowly.

"Please?" David asked, realizing what my answer was going to be.

"I . . . I can't, David. I'm sorry but this is just too much for me."

"But I love you." He tried to take my hand.

I pulled it away.

"Leave, David."

"Janelle . . ."

"Please leave," I said again. I turned away from him and went to the window. I didn't want to see him anymore. I couldn't bear it. I stood holding on to the roses he'd given me, while he stood behind me. Neither one of us said a word.

We stayed that way for a few minutes until I heard David sigh.

"I'll call the movers for you. Goodbye, Janelle."

I turned and watched David walk to the door. I wanted to call out to him and tell him not to leave, that I wanted to give things another try. But instead I watched him walk through the door and out of my life.

David

Goodbye.

That was the most difficult thing I'd ever had to say. I really thought Janelle would give me another chance. We'd experienced some highs and extreme lows, yet we always managed to find our way back to one another. I thought we would do the same this time. I thought we were going to survive. I was almost sure of it. But I guess I underestimated what I'd put her through. My lies. My betrayal. My immaturity. It was just too much.

After I called and paid for the moving company to come and take Janelle's things, I walked aimlessly. I had no destination and didn't care to find one. I walked, reminiscing about when Janelle and I first met and when she said yes to my proposal. Those moments eclipsed anything that I had or thought I had with Jocelyn. I'd never match the intensity of my feelings for Jocelyn, but the love she and I shared would never be as strong as what Janelle and I had. I just wished I'd realized that before I made the decisions I'd made. Had I never sent that e-mail, things would have been different. Maybe Isaiah would never have died.

I walked, oblivious to the hustle and bustle all around me. I looked at my watch. *Janelle would be leaving soon.* I walked alone, time passing slowly and quickly at the same time. I looked at my watch again. *Janelle had left.* I guess it was time for me to move on.

"You all right, bruh?" Marc asked, smiling from ear to ear. It was his wedding day, and he and Dahlia had just had finished their official first dance together as husband and wife. I was sitting at the wedding party table. I'd been there since we'd first arrived at the reception.

I was happy for both Marc and Dahlia, and I wanted to join in on the revelry of their big day, but I just couldn't because it made me think about Janelle and what we used to have. I hadn't seen or heard from her since I left her apartment, which was a little over a year ago.

During that time I thought about her constantly. So much so that I didn't even have the desire to date. I tried to call her a few times and left messages at her job and at her parents' home, but she never returned any of my calls.

I wanted to fly out to California to try and see her, but once my new book hit the shelves, I had no free time. The book, which I'd based on what happened between Janelle and me was a huge success, making the *New York Times* Best Seller list. I often wondered if Janelle ever picked up a copy. If she did, she'd see in words what she truly meant to me. In my book, the woman took the man back. I guess that's where the fiction took over.

Marc's wedding was a happy, monumentous occasion, and as much as I tried to not let it be, it was a very painful slap in the face reminding me of what I threw away.

"Yeah, I'm cool," I said.

A couple of guests came by to offer their congratulations to Marc. When they walked away he raised his eyebrows and sighed. "Man, can you believe I am officially out of the game?"

"I'm still having a hard time with that one," I said, smiling.

"I'm locked up, bruh. The ball and chain has been clasped around my ankle, the key thrown away, the spare broken, and the spare to the spare melted down to liquid. A life sentence, bruh."

"You allowed visitors?"

"Yeah, but only the male kind—heterosexual, of course."

"I'd hope so."

Marc and I laughed.

If there was any one thing I could rely on, it was Marc's ability to lift my spirits. "You know you do have the right to an appeal," I said.

"This is true. But you only get that approved if you've been on good behavior. And once Dahlia and I hop into the limo to leave for the Caymans, my chances are pretty much shot."

We laughed again, and then another couple of guests stopped by. Marc shook their hands, said, "Thank you," and then gave me a smirk. I could tell he was loving every moment of his moment. "Only a few more hours," he said.

"Yeah. So you're really happy, huh?"

"Bruh, *happy* is not the word. I'm so far up Dahlia's ass it's ridiculous. I love that woman." He paused and looked over at the dance floor, where Dahlia was getting her groove on with her six-year-old niece, Tatiana. "She's the shit, man."

I threw my arm over his shoulder. "I'm happy for you, man. Really happy. What you and Dahlia have is special and something to envy."

Marc smiled. "Yeah, it is."

We sat silent for a couple of seconds and listened to the music being played by the DJ. Everyone was out on the dance floor now jamming to Beyonce's song, "Crazy In Love."

"You know," Marc said, breaking the silence, "this is gonna be you some day."

I shrugged my shoulders. "I don't know, man. I don't think I want to head down the road again. I may have to adopt your old philosophy."

"Bruh, please. You know that's not happening. I was born a playa-playa. Emphasis on the *was*. You are, have always been, and will always be a lover-lover. Man, you had a bad experience with Janelle."

"I fucked up, man."

"All right, you fucked up. But Dave, man, look out on that dance floor and tell me what you see."

I looked to the dance floor but Marc didn't wait for my answer.

"I'll tell you what you see, bruh—women. No, not just women. Fine women. Fine, single, of age, accomplished, independent, experienced women. Bruh, you haven't dated one female since Janelle left. If you weren't my boy I'd be a little frightened. I know the whole Janelle-Jocelyn episode hurts, but you need to start fishing again. No, damn that, you need to get rid of the pole and jump right in the water and go find you some fish. Hell, find a mermaid. They're already naked and waiting."

I laughed out loud. "You're insane. You know that, right?"

"Yeah, I know. Seriously, man, this is supposed to be my celebration. But how can I do that if my best friend, my best man, my brother, is sitting here sulking?" Marc looked at me and raised an eyebrow.

"My bad, man," I said.

Marc stood up. "Hey, don't apologize. Just get your ass up and come out onto the dance floor and start swimming." He walked away without saying anything else. He went to the dance floor, jumped right behind Dahlia and started grooving in step with her.

I smiled. He was right. I needed to swim. I looked out at the floor at the other women shaking their thangs. My eyes stopped on a chocolate-brown female with a dancer's body and Toni Braxton hair . . . before the weave.

She looked at me and flashed a "Janet Jackson" smile.

I stood up and jumped into the sea.

Janelle

I closed the book and sighed. David had just finished speaking to me through his latest book. I wasn't going to buy it. I'd seen it so many times in the bookstores, but I avoided it just like I'd been avoiding him since I told him to leave.

After I moved back home to California, I forced myself to move on. I took a senior editor's position with another major publishing house and threw myself into my work.

When I wasn't working, I did some major catch up with Tina's crazy behind. She and I hung out and did a lot of the things we used to do before I moved away. Tina helped me come to grips with Isaiah's death, and she also helped me deal with David's goodbye.

"Girl, you don't need his ass and you can find a better man. One who deserves what you have to offer."

Those were her words of wisdom any time I brought up David's name.

Eventually I bought into her philosophy and started to date occasionally. I wasn't desperate or needy, but maybe Tina was right.

My first few dates were complete nightmares. I had one

brother planning our wedding after a night out to the movies. Another brother invited me out to a fancy restaurant and then couldn't pay for the bill. I even had one fool try to take me out for a night on the town in his pink Cadillac. Needless to say, that wasn't much of a date because I never got in the car. My string of dating nightmares really had me missing the comfort and companionship of a real relationship.

I was about to forsake dating completely, when I met Mahlon. He was the man I'd been seeing for the past three months. He was a nice guy. A guidance counselor at a high school, he was grounded, secure and could carry on a mean conversation. He wasn't as handsome as David, but he's not bad. The nice thing about Mahlon was that, like myself, he'd been burned by love, so he was all for taking things slowly. And that was good because slow was the only way I was willing to go.

We didn't see each other all the time, which was a good thing. Maybe once or twice during the week, but mostly on the weekends.

I was supposed to see him in a few hours.

But then I read the book.

Damn the book.

I closed my eyes and sat back in my chair, the story, our story playing in my mind. He'd poured his heart into the tale. No one else may realize that, but I did. And I know that's what he wanted. Was it still possible? Could that road be traveled again? I thought about Mahlon, or at least tried to. But David boldly kicked him out of the picture.

I picked up the book and held it in my hands. It was hardback and filled with meaning. I opened it to the last page, where I said how much I loved David and how much I wanted to give our love another try. Then David and I embraced. The end.

I put the book down and reached for my laptop—yes, I had one now. I started typing.

David

David,

I am sure that if you weren't already sitting, you are now. Believe me, that I am writing you is as much a shock to me as it is to you. I don't even know where to start. I suppose hello would be appropriate. This is awkward. I still can't believe I'm doing this. I should just stop typing and put this damn laptop away. Yes, I have my own laptop now. And no, my fingers won't stop. I wish they would though. After the shit you put me through, I swore I wouldn't talk to you again. I got all of the messages you left for me. As you can see, I had no intention of returning any of them. I forced myself to move on and live my life, looking for a man that deserved everything I had to offer him. That's what I was doing, David. Living my life. I found a way to be happy again. And I found a man who treats me the way I want and need to be treated. He's a good man who genuinely cares about my needs. I was successful in moving on David. I was on my way to finding something called happiness. Or at least contentment.

And then I read your book.

I started it yesterday and finished it today. Damn you,

David. I didn't want to read the book. I didn't want to have anything to do with you. I remember the day the book was released. There was so much talk about it here at work. I know my parents told you, but I'm senior editor for another major publishing house. Anyway, there was a lot of talk about your book. People actually went to buy a copy. But not me. Like I said, I didn't want to read the book. I didn't want to see your words. I didn't want to be taken back to the place I desperately ran away from. So whenever I'd see your book, I'd avoid it. I wouldn't even take a glance at the cover. I didn't want to see your name. But yesterday I was at Borders, not looking for your book, but looking for a different book. Any book. But not yours. Like I always do when I go to Borders, I took a look at the upcoming events for the month and I saw your name. Your picture. Your smile. I didn't want to, but I read what you had scheduled. You're coming to the store in two weeks for a signing. I tried not to care. You were coming-so what. I moved on and went to go and find a book to read. I went through the shelves quickly at first, nothing really catching my eye. But then I slowed down. And then I stopped moving past the books altogether. And when I did, I realized that I had stopped in front of your book. I need to stop typing. I really do. I also needed to stop my hands from moving to the shelf to grab a copy. But I didn't.

Damn you, David.

I went home and paced, trying to get myself to take the book back to the store, give it away, throw it away. Anything. I just didn't want to sit down with a cup of hot tea, curl up on the couch, and read your damn book. But that's just what I did at twelve o'clock in the morning. I went to bed at four. Came to work at nine. Finished the book by three this afternoon.

Damn you, David.

I spent all this time moving past you. Forgetting about everything that happened between us and here you went and wrote a beautiful story. Our story. You spoke directly to me through your words. Damn you for making me remember every-thing that we shared, how good the love was. The love that I tried so hard to get past, but never really could, no matter how much I lied to myself and said I did. I have to say it again, it was a truly beautiful story. It pulled me in from the word go and forced me to listen loud and clear. I heard you, David. You were in the room with me, whispering into my ears. Now I want you to listen. I will never forget what you did to me, David. Never. And honestly, I don't want to. Remembering your lies and your deceit have made me a stronger woman. I'm not a fool anymore. Are you paying attention? I'm not a fool. I want you to remember that. Because all you'll get from me is this second chance. I hope you make it count like you did in our book. I'll see you at the signing. I love you.

I logged off of my e-mail and then closed my laptop. And then I sat. Stunned. Speechless. And on the verge of jumping up and down for joy.

She e-mailed me. She read the book. She wanted to give us another try.

I closed my eyes and smiled. *She e-mailed me.* Sade was playing from my stereo. This was déjà vu. But it was much better the second time around.

Reading Group Guide

1. David and Jocelyn were each other's first love. Had David never cheated, do you think they would have still been together?
2. What would you have done in Marc's and Marisol's position? Would you have lied for David and Jocelyn?
3. Do you think Jocelyn truly loved David?
4. If you had been in Janelle's position, would you have checked David's laptop after Tina put the bug in her ear about the possibility of David cheating?
5. Do you still think about your first love? And if given the chance, would you rekindle the flame that once existed?
6. How did you feel about Jocelyn's reaction to Isaiah's death?
7. David was willing to throw away his relationship with Janelle to be with Jocelyn. Did he really love Janelle?
8. Why do you think Eric took Jocelyn back?
9. Did Jocelyn get what she deserved, when Eric left at the end?
10. How do you feel about Janelle taking David back at the end?

Enjoy a sample chapter from
Dwayne S. Joseph's next novel

In Too Deep

Abe

"Give me another fifteen minutes, and I'll really give you something to smile about."

"Believe me, Taki, if I had fifteen more minutes to spare, and another pair of boxers with me, it would be on."

"You were incredible today, Abe. I can still feel you inside of me."

"That's what I like to hear."

"Ten more minutes?" Taki begged, placing her hand over my crotch.

It wasn't easy to do, but I grabbed a hold of her hand and pulled it away from my hardening member. "We both need to get home, Taki."

"Five more minutes?" she said, grabbing hold of me again with her other hand. "Put it in. Give me a few good, hard thrusts, and then pull it out. I want to feel you inside of me again."

"Don't get greedy, Taki," I said, pulling her other hand away, which had nearly succeeded in getting my zipper all the way down. "Being greedy will only ruin things."

Taki moaned and nibbled on my ear lobe. "It's hard to not be greedy, Abe," she said with a whisper.

"But it's better to be safe than sorry."

Taki groaned. "I'm tired of being safe."

"But for your kids you will be."

Taki sighed. "I know."

"Get home," I said. "I'll see you tomorrow."

"Okay," she said reluctantly.

We kissed for a few seconds and then got in our cars and drove away to go back to our separate lives.

Things were starting to change. Well, Taki was. I'd been noticing it the past few times we'd been together, but really saw it this time. The longer, tighter hugs. The lingering of her lips on mine for far longer than they should be. The look in her eyes that no longer growled, "Come and fuck me," but now whispered, "Come and lay with me." I had hoped this wouldn't happen. Taki had caught feelings.

I tightened my grip around my steering wheel and clenched my jaws. I'd been seeing Taki for a little over seven months. We'd first made eye contact at a company Christmas party. She'd been there with her husband Whilice. I was there with my wife Nakyia. Taki was working in a different department at the time, but a month after the party, she was promoted to be the head of the entire East Coast region of advertising. I began working under her a month after that.

Everything was on the up-and-up in the beginning. We were both two very driven individuals who took pride in creating television and print ad campaigns that drove consumers toward the client's product. Nextel, Sean John, Nike—these were just a few of the companies that relied on our flavor. Taki and I made a great team. With her visual skills and my flair for creating catchy slogans and witty dialogue, companies were practically battling to render our services.

Like I said, in the beginning our relationship was strictly

business. I won't lie and say that we never flirted or exchanged glances here and there, because we did. But we were both married, so we never let the flirtation go too far. But one day out of the blue, sitting in her office trying to come up with an ad campaign for a Latino-owned clothing company, without warning, Taki changed the dynamics of our relationship.

I was in mid-sentence reciting a slogan I'd come up with, when Taki reached across the table we'd been sitting by and placed her lips against mine. Taken by surprise, I pulled back almost immediately. Almost. I won't lie, I did take a moment to taste the cherry lipstick she'd been wearing. But it had only been a moment.

"What was that about?"

Taki looked at me for a few short seconds and licked her lips sensuously. Then she said, "One of us had to make the move."

" 'The move'?"

"Yes."

"What do you mean?"

"You know what I mean, Abe."

I clenched my jaws for a second and then nodded. She was right; I did know.

"This was going to happen sooner or later," she said. "There was no point in delaying the inevitable. I'm actually surprised that you didn't move first."

"You're married," I said, thinking about all of the times I'd imagined doing just that."

"So are you," Taki countered.

"You're also my boss," I said. "The whole Michael Douglas-Demi Moore scenario in *Disclosure* isn't one I'd like to experience."

"Trust me, Abe . . . I may be finer than Demi, but I am nowhere near as crazy as her character was."

I flashed a slight smile. Half Asian, half black, with an Angela Bassett physique, Lauryn Hill lips, and eyes that could make the gayest of men turn straight, I had to agree—Demi in her heyday couldn't touch Taki on her worst.

I stroked my goatee. "Demi didn't lose her mind until Mike gave it to her," I said.

Taki smirked. "Are you saying you'll make me lose my mind, Abe?"

I shook my head. "I'm just saying that Demi was sane until she got dicked down."

Taki's eyes closed a bit as she nibbled down on her bottom lip. "Are you going to dick me down?" she asked, coming around the table and standing in front of me. "Is that what you plan to do? Make me crazy? Do you have skills like that?"

Taki traced a finely manicured index finger down my cheek to my chest, and then down to my crotch.

My hand found its way beneath both her blouse and bra. "In my twenty-eight years," I said, squeezing her erect nipple, "I've never had any complaints. And I've always had requests for thirds and fourths."

Taki let out a slow breath and moaned. "But will you make me go crazy?" she asked, pulling my zipper down, slipping past my boxers and grabbing hold of me.

I closed my eyes and got chills as she stroked.

"You're so big, Abe," Taki whispered.

"Still want to know if I'll make you crazy?" I asked as my tongue did circles around her nipple now.

"Since I first laid my eyes on you at the company party," Taki said breathlessly.

No need for further conversation, Taki and I undressed and then fucked on top of the work we had spread out across the round, sturdy table. I answered Taki's question with every deep, hard thrust. Answered it so good that she demanded I go deeper, harder, faster, until she orgasmed.

When we were finished, Taki took a finger, dipped it in

the semen I'd spilled across her stomach, and took that finger into her mouth. "Good answer," she said with a seductive smile.

Wiping myself off with my T-shirt, I asked the first question that popped into my mind when I released. "You don't plan on doing a Demi to me now, do you, boss?"

"Cut the boss bullshit," Taki said. "I told you, I'm not crazy. But . . ." she paused, licked her lips, and then said, "your dick is good."

Things were never the same after that.

Never letting the pleasure come before the business, Taki and I fucked whenever and wherever we could. In her office. In mine. In the backseat of her car. In the front seat of mine. At a hotel. Sometimes on the way there.

I know I should have felt guilty about what was going on. After all, my wife, Nakyia was a beautiful 5'5, slender, yet thick in all of the right places. Beautiful brown eyes to go with her smooth, coffee-colored skin. Short, Toni Braxton hairstyle to complement her soft, round face. Educated with the perfect combination of book and common sense. I'd be hard pressed to find a woman as complete as Nakyia was.

Being riddled with guilt was definitely something that I should have been, but I wasn't. See, as perfect as Nakyia was, there was just one imperfect thing about her. Something that was completely out of her control.

Two years before Taki came into the picture, Nakyia was afflicted with trigeminal neuralgia, a disorder of the fifth cranial, or trigeminal nerve that causes episodes of intense, stabbing, electric shock-like pain in the areas of the face where the branches of the nerve are distributed. Lips, eyes, nose, scalp, forehead, upper and lower jaw—the whole right side of her face was affected. Universally considered to be one of the most painful afflictions known to man, trigeminal neuralgia isn't fatal, but it is an extremely painful and life-changing disorder.

Because of the constant pain she was in, the intimacy in our marriage disappeared. We couldn't caress the same, couldn't kiss with the same passion as we used to. Worst of all, the sex changed. One minute Nakyia would be fine, and the next minute, she'd be damn near tears from the pain searing through the right side of her face.

It was frustrating to watch the woman I loved suffer, and not be able to do anything about it. So frustrating, that after a while, I completely gave up on trying to have any intimacy at all. With the distance the neuralgia caused, we went from living together as husband and wife to nothing more than roommates who occasionally slept together in the same bed. And I say occasionally because I spent many nights out on the couch because it was just too damned hard to be in the same bed without being able to touch her.

I know that to a lot of people my affair with Taki was just plain wrong. After all, Nakyia was suffering. She was the one forced to take medicine four times a day with little relief. She was the one who couldn't talk without feeling pain, couldn't eat without feeling pain, couldn't walk without the wind blowing on her face and causing her to cringe and clench her jaws as she fought tears and willed the pain to go away.

She was the one who had trigeminal neuralgia.

Not me.

I was just the bystander, and having an affair was just about the lowest thing to do. Bystander or not, I vowed through sickness and health, and I was supposed to be the rock for Nakyia to lean on. That's what anyone standing on the outside looking in would say, and they would be right. Cheating was wrong.

But until they've walked in my shoes, they would never understand how doing the wrong thing was something that I desperately needed to do, because they would never be able to fully grasp the depths of my frustration over not being able to kiss or caress my wife without the knowledge that the pleasure I was trying to bring her could and often times did bring her nothing but pain.

But our sex life or better yet—lack of one—wasn't the only thing that pushed me into another woman's arms. Four times a day, every day, Nakyia had no choice but to take medication, just so that she could function on a somewhat normal level. Because of the medicine, she developed some nasty mood swings, and most of the time I did whatever I could to avoid being around her. But even when she was almost herself, and I wanted nothing more than to just be by her side, nothing for us was normal. We rarely went out in public together or hung out with friends because she felt embarrassed by her condition. We couldn't do normal things like take showers together, because the water hitting her face would cause her pain. We couldn't laugh together the same way we used to, because she could never just let go.

Nothing was the same for us anymore.

Like I said, cheating was wrong and I knew it. But I'm human. And as the distance between Nakyia grew wider, I began to get lonely. I missed the affection. I missed the excitement of being a couple in love with nothing but the usual worries. When Taki laid that kiss on me, as much I wanted to fight it, the urge to be physical without holding back was just too strong, and I enjoyed all that Taki had to give and gave her all that she could take.

The regret never came.

And I only wanted more.

As I drove home, I thought about the arrangement Taki and I had made. We agreed to satisfy each other's urges and give each other the attention neither of us got at home, without expectations.

No strings attached in the truest form.

I tightened my grip around my steering wheel even harder and blew out a frustrated breath of air through my nostrils. Taki had caught feelings, and I was going to have to change that. I was happy with the arrangement we had and saw no reason for a change.